the black canary

the
black
canary

JANE LOUISE CURRY

Margaret K. McElderry Books
New York   London   Toronto   Sydney

Margaret K. McElderry Books
An imprint of Simon & Schuster Children's Publishing Division
1230 Avenue of the Americas, New York, New York 10020
Book design by Kristin Smith
The text for this book is set in Goudy.
Manufactured in the United States of America
10 9 8 7 6 5 4
Library of Congress Cataloging-in-Publication Data
Curry, Jane Louise.
The Black Canary / Jane Louise Curry.—1st ed.
p. cm.
Summary: Twelve-year-old James has no interest in music in spite of the
fact that both his parents are musicians, but when he discovers a portal
to seventeenth-century London in his uncle's basement, he finds that
his beautiful voice and the fact that he is biracial might serve him well.
ISBN 0-689-86478-7 (hardcover)
1. London (England)—History—17th century—Juvenile fiction.
2. Great Britain—History—Elizabeth, 1558–1603—Juvenile fiction.
3. Essex, Robert Devereux, Earl of, 1566–1601—Juvenile fiction.
[1. London (England)—History—17th century—Fiction. 2. Great
Britain—History—Elizabeth, 1558–1603—Fiction. 3. Time travel—
Fiction. 4. Racially mixed people—Fiction. 5. Singing—Fiction.
6. Essex, Robert Devereux, Earl of, 1566–1601—Fiction.] I. Title.
PZ7.C936Bl 2005
[Fic]—dc22
2003026150

For Margaret McElderry,
with love

*"The exercise of singing is delightfull to Nature,
and good to preserve health of Man."*
—William Byrd, 1588

one

AT FIRST, JAMES THOUGHT HE WAS AWAKE. He opened his eyes into inky darkness and lay quite still, scarcely breathing, his heart fluttering as if something had frightened him. Even as fuzzy as his thinking was, that seemed silly. Alarmed him, then. Had he heard something? A sound? Water? If it were his granddad making his usual middle-of-the-night visit to the bathroom, he would have recognized the familiar faint knocking and gurgling from the pipes in his grandparents' side of the old house. A "duplex," the house was called back when most of the houses in their Pittsburgh neighborhood were built like that: two houses stuck together like Siamese twins. Besides, gurgling pipes might wake him but wouldn't *frighten* him awake. James floated on the surface of sleep, but the lingering sense of fright, of wrongness, kept him from slipping out of the dark, silent room and back into his dream. Thoughts of what might have alarmed him were wisps of fog, stirring and moving away as he reached for them.

He peered at the window and saw that an almost invisible bloom of light rimmed the window blind. The house was wrapped in middle-of-the-night stillness, but perhaps morning was already creeping closer. He always kept his watch on at night so he wouldn't have to grope for it on the nightstand, and with an effort he raised his wrist and pressed the tiny button on its left side. The watch-face light blinked on. Twenty-five minutes past two. So the dim light at the window wasn't morning on the way after all. And the distant thread of sound that had crept into his dream and still murmured at the edge of hearing? It *was* water, but not water gurgling through pipes. *Running* water. If he held his breath he could still hear it, faint but as clear as if it were running inside his head.

Spilling over a sink, he thought lazily. Spreading across

a floor, seeping downward, running down a wall . . .

Spilling over a sink! James's eyes blinked open. He would have scrambled up and switched on the bedside lamp but, to his slow surprise, found he could not move. His hands and arms were leaden, and his legs like dreaming logs of stone, as if gravity were pulling him down through the mattress. With a great effort he rolled sideways to lie on his back, and fought to keep his eyes open. The water would seep down through the ceiling of the dining room, and the plaster would crack, and the chandelier with glass leaves and flowers would crash down onto the dining room table. What if he could not move until morning? The gray light would not come for hours to creep its slow way around the white walls, bringing each of his treasures to life. First it would touch the bright Kwanzaa postage stamp in its postcard-sized frame on the near wall, then the end wall with the CD jewel case with the cover photo of his mama. Her brown skin glowed against her gold gown, and he loved the way her eyes shone as if someone had just told a great joke and she was trying not to laugh. Next the light would touch the tiny figure of a Buffalo Soldier atop his bookshelf. The soldier, cast in one of Granddad Hackaday's moulds and painted by James himself, stood beside Grandpa Parrett's almost-as-tiny wood carving of a chickadee. Both were gifts for his twelfth birthday, almost a year ago now.

The CD was *Shareen Parrett Sings Arne, Purcell, and Dowland.* James had put it up in place of the big old poster of his parents—*Jazz at the Blue Dolphin: Reenie Hackaday, with Phil Parrett at the Piano & the Tommy Mann Trio*—that had hung there since he was six. The Kwanzaa poster Grandma had first put up had been a beautiful poster of the same Kwanzaa postage stamp that was there now, but at least four feet across, and *bright.* Even in the dark it felt like having the Preservation Hall Jazz Band jamming, or an orchestra blaring Sousa marches in his bedroom. "But honey, your poor room looks so *bare* now," Grandma had protested as she rolled the two posters up together and James filled a box with things to go to the attic.

No, it looks nice, James thought fuzzily. *Cool.* Falling asleep was much easier with the calmer walls.

Sky blue walls. Three clouds painted on the ceiling. Tidy bookshelves . . .

His eyes flew open.

Sky blue walls . . . That was what was wrong. These weren't sky blue. He couldn't see them, but he was sure of it. And this room was larger than his. Emptier. He could hear the difference even in the silence. Really. Once when he was small, at his white grandparents' house in Maine, he had shrieked out in the middle of the night that he heard a spider walking around under his bed, and a sleepy Grandpa Parrett had told him he was dreaming. When a look under the bed with a flashlight showed a very real spider walking around, Grandpa had got rid of it and said, "James, your ears must be as amazing as your eyes. Next thing we know, you'll be leaping over tall buildings with a single bound!"

Slowly James remembered where he was. These walls had pale green and cream stripes, with framed old prints of animals and birds, and no doors leading on the one side into his own upstairs hall and on the other into his grandparents' side of the old duplex house. He wasn't in his own room at home in Pittsburgh at all. He was in England. Since noon yesterday. And this was the back bedroom in Cousin Charles Parrett's apartment in Clerkenwell Close, in London. Cousin Charles was in Italy for the summer and James and his parents were in his apartment. In London.

Where he was miserable. Where he did *not* want to be.

And where there really was water running somewhere.

The sound was so faint, at the very edge of hearing, that James was sure it couldn't be from the next-door bathroom, where he had very definitely turned the water off after brushing his teeth. That left the other bathroom, he thought muzzily, or the kitchen sink overflowing, or even a leak inside the walls.

James sat up, this time with no trouble at all, and swung his feet to the thick, soft bedside rug. He reached down to pick up his sneakers and, because the air was cool, groped around the top of the sheet and then on the floor for his pajamas, which his mother always put out, even though he never wore them in summer. Still a little fuzzy-headed with sleep, he felt his way past the foot of the bed to the wall, and moved from there to the door and out along the hallway's cool, polished floor to the bathroom next door.

The taps in both the basin and tub *were* firmly off. Not even a drip dropped from the showerhead. James moved on down the hall, carrying the shoes and trailing his pajama top, and pressed his ear to the wall of the bathroom off the bedroom where his parents slept. Nothing. Nor was there any leak, drip, or water running in the sleek, stainless-steel kitchen. James's bare feet made a light slapping sound on the tiled kitchen floor as he turned back toward the hallway and the sitting room. They carried him across nubbly carpet into the wide entryway and left him standing at the front door. The darkness all around him was filled with silence, but under the silence the water still murmured, tantalizing, almost not there.

He unlocked the door and stepped out onto the landing. Cousin Charles's apartment was on the top floor of a building of offices and workshops in Clerkenwell Close, and it had its own staircase. James had four dimly lit flights to pad down. At the foot of the bottom stair he followed the sound back along the shadowy hallway at the side of the staircase. An ordinary paneled door waited at the far end, and as James leaned forward to press an ear against one of its oak panels, he heard the same elusive murmur of water, so he turned the knob and pushed the door open. The sound of water was suddenly as clear and thin and cold as a freshwater spring. Odder still, the air, too, held a sharp chill.

Warily—thinking of spiders—James felt along the wall just inside the door for a light switch, then along the other side, but there was none to be found. Shivering, he pulled on his pajama top and peered into the darkness. In the dim light coming from the front-door end of the hallway, he could make out a stair stepping downward and, directly ahead at eye level, a faint gray line leading upward. A pull cord for a light? Curiosity drew James downward, but he was stepping into his own shadow and could not see where to put his feet, so he had to feel his way. The first step below turned out to be cold, gritty concrete, and automatically

James sat down on the top step to pull on his shoes. *Of course*, he thought sleepily. *That's why I brought them.* When he stood, he gripped the iron handrail and felt mistrustfully for the next tread. With each step he stopped to fish for the light cord in the dark air ahead until it brushed his fingertips and he could snatch at it.

A small naked bulb blinked on. James peered around and saw the bare concrete floor and white-painted concrete block walls of an ordinary basement. To the left of the stair, three rubbish bins were lined up along the wall. Along the right-hand wall he saw a large, gas-fired central-heating boiler, a deep janitor's sink beside it, and half a dozen large, empty wooden tea chests stacked in one corner. He saw no drip from the sink's tap, but still heard the thin but steady sound of water falling into a basin. Peering back toward the shadowy far corner to his left, where the sound seemed to come from, for a moment he thought he saw a faint oval shimmer hanging motionless in midair. The shape was more a stirring in the air than a shine or gleam, but James's imagination shied away at the thought. *A reflection.* That was it. *Or a shadow on the white-painted concrete blocks . . .*

The light bulb gave a faint *pop!* and went dark.

In the sudden darkness the oval *something* in the air was still there, but clearer and hovering like a gray glimmer of mist in a warm night. Through it James thought he saw a patch of gray stone wall instead of the painted concrete blocks he had seen with the light on. He stared blankly for a long moment. He rubbed his eyes. The patch did not go away.

James wavered for a moment between alarm and curiosity, then drew a shaky breath and took a cautious step forward in the darkness. At each step the strange oval appeared to grow wider, as if it were . . . morphing into a circle. James hesitated. What if whatever it was suddenly yawned wide and swallowed him? He twitched back a little and, when he did, it shrank, and he realized that if he didn't move, it didn't. He took a step back, then another forward. As he did, the faint shimmer that stirred in the cold air narrowed a step's worth, and then widened again.

Curiouser and curiouser, James thought, feeling a

lot like Alice at the rabbit hole. He turned a little to the right and moved cautiously toward what he thought would be the rear wall. As he did, the mysterious shape grew still narrower, until it was no more than a thin line in the darkness. Another step, and it vanished. Half a step back, and it was there again: an uncertain thread of not-quite light that glimmered on and off. James took a long step toward the back wall, keeping an eye on the spot where the line vanished. There it was again! Baffled, he moved still farther around to the left until he found himself facing another, brighter circle of shimmer in the darkness.

It took a moment for James to realize that the light he saw was not in the circle itself, but what lay beyond it. He was facing a dim view of a worn stone step, with a narrow landing just above, and a dark, arched doorway into the stone wall or building to his left. Beyond was another, shallower stair. At the top, the silhouettes of leafless trees stood out black against the moon-bright sky. The air held both the last faint bite of winter and the moist, earthy scent of early spring. He could see every silhouetted tree twig, and hear their faint clatter as they stirred in a whisper of breeze. Most dreamily strange of all, James could see at the same time both the moonlit stone steps in front of him and—outside of and beyond and above the eerie circle—the open door at the top of Cousin Charles's basement steps and the warmer glow from the light in the ground-floor entry hall. He was still in the *here*, but not three feet away was a *there*.

James stood motionless. *This is a dream*, he realized in a rush of relief and disappointment. He had been excited as much as fearful, and even though he shivered a little from the cold, he thought, *Don't let me wake up. Not yet. Not yet.* He did not understand what he was seeing. How could the stone wall he had glimpsed from the other side of the circle be the same stone wall that rose at the side of the moonlit stair in front of him? He sidled around to the other side of the window in the air and watched the same thing happen as he went: His view of the circle dwindled to an oval, the oval to a line as thin as a thread of spider silk that shimmers on and off in dappled sunlight, and that line widening back into a shadowy circle. From either side the circle looked, more than anything, like—like exactly that: a window in the air. A window with faintly frosted glass. James edged a little nearer to peer into its shadows.

Beyond the misty shimmer a sloping passage ran down between stone walls, shadowy on one side, moonlit on the other. The passage stair led downward through what James knew was—what he squatted down and *felt* was—a solid concrete floor. At the bottom of that stair he could dimly make out a door. When he inched even closer and leaned forward to peer at the shimmer, his forehead touched it, and he jerked back. The touch of it was . . . *fizzy*, like electricity in his hair. Close up, the look of it was gently fizzy too. He touched his finger to it and snatched it back again. The tip of his finger tingled a little, but it looked and felt fine. Moving around until all he could see of the circle was the thin edge, he stuck his left hand in on the downstairs side, then his right in on the upper landing side, and tried to grasp one hand with the other.

Both hands disappeared up to the wrists. They

vanished, and no matter how he waggled them in the cold air, or where he groped, they did not meet. If he leaned around to look, he could see the one on that side, but not the other. And vice versa. His stomach gave an unpleasant lurch, but when he pulled his hands out again, both were fine except for the faint tingle.

James took a deep breath, leaned forward, and thrust his face through the pale fizz.

A colder draft of air from below brushed past his face, and with it came—much more clearly—the sound of water spilling into a basin. Without thinking, he stepped forward to feel with a foot for the stone step below, only to have his foot jar against the concrete floor and to find himself still in Cousin Charles's basement, on the far side of the window in the air. He had walked straight through it and could feel the almost-not-there tingle from his hips up.

James turned and stared up for a moment at the other-world landing one step above. *Okay. It's like a window. You don't try to walk through a wall to get out through the window in that wall. You climb over the sill.*

With the growing sharpness of his eyes in the dark

and the faint light from the shimmer, James was able to make out the dim shapes of the wooden tea chests stacked in the corner beyond the gas-fired boiler, just beyond a pair of rubbish bins. Moving cautiously, arms outstretched, he crossed to the corner and pulled one of the boxes to the floor. Its size and smooth sides made it a little awkward to pick up and clumsy to carry, but he struggled with it across to the back side of the shimmer. If you were going to climb through a window with nothing to hold on to, you didn't want to pitch yourself down a flight of stone steps. You would climb *up*, to the landing.

The tea chest had no top, so James turned it to stand bottom up and tested to see whether it would hold his weight. Then he took a deep breath, climbed on top, and crouched down to edge sideways through the shimmer.

Like launching yourself through a keyhole . . .

two

JAMES REACHED OUT TO THE WALL TO STEADY himself as he stepped up to the landing and pushed himself erect. For a long minute the only sound he heard was his own heart thumping wildly. It took an even longer minute before he could uproot his feet from the stone floor to turn and look behind him. He was in the roofed-over portion of a stairwell next to a building. Above the landing the rest of the stair was open to the sky and full of moonlight. Shivering, James touched the stone wall and marveled at the dream. The faint shimmer rested on the step below him, and looking down through it, all he could see of his own world was a misty shadow of an upended tea chest, and darkness beyond. He edged close to the wall so that he could look past the tingle in the air to the next stone step below and squeeze downward without touching it.

Once past, James saw that the steps were steep and old, worn to a dip in the middle. Trailing his hand along the wall for balance, he followed the sound of water down into the shadows. Three steps beyond the foot of the stairs was a door with a peep-slot cut into it. As he moved toward it, his foot stubbed against an object that turned out to be a wooden bucket with a short length of rope coiled like a snake at its bottom. He shoved it to one side and stretched up on tiptoe to peer through the man-high peep-slot, but he wasn't tall enough to see any more than a patch of night sky.

The door was closed by an iron bar supported on the left by a bracket set into the door frame, and on the right end fastened to a heavy ring-and-staple hinge. The bar lifted easily, and James guessed that the heavy iron pin hanging on a cord just below the hinge was meant to be fitted into a hole in the door frame, so as to prop the bar up and out of the way while the door was open. The shadows in the stairwell were so deep that he had to fumble around with cold fingers to find the hole. With the bar up and the pin in place, the heavy door moved easily at a tug on its iron-ring handle, rumbling only a little along the stone floor. James took a cautious look outside, then opened it wide enough to squeeze through.

He found himself standing three steps above the water of a stone-walled well, or pool, that had been built against the outer wall of the building. The mysterious sound he had followed was the water that welled from a spring somewhere up the slope under the building, for it spilled from a pipe set into the wall five or six feet above the pool. Beyond the foot of the well was a road, pale in the moonlight, that on the right ran gently upward toward open fields. On the left the road slid down into shadow. Directly across, three moonlit houses huddled close together. But Cousin Charles's flat was surrounded for miles by London's sprawl. So where was this? Silly question. It was a dream. It was Nowhere.

James shivered in the chilly air and suddenly remembered to button his pajama top. The dream road and the moonlit fields were tantalizing, but the air was too cold for him to be tempted out of the sheltering doorway. Even so, cold or not, he was too enchanted by the stillness and the strangeness to retreat. He crouched down to sit on his heels with his back against the doorjamb and his arms around his knees and marvel at the strange stillness and emptiness of this new world.

At home there were times he would give anything for stillness and a little peaceful emptiness.

Here there was no Grandma sweeping in through the Hackaday door to his bedroom like a billowy, warm whirlwind that took your breath away. He loved her dearly, but he was almost *thirteen*, so why couldn't she leave him alone at home when she had to play the organ for a choir rehearsal, instead of whisking him off to Cousin Alvah's for safekeeping? When she took him shopping, it never failed: Before he could reach for a T-shirt he liked, she would pull out a wild swirl of blue and orange and purple, hold it up against him, and sweep him and the shirt off to the cash register. Or at home it had been that voice like dark velvet calling up the stairs, "James, honey, you pull your nose out of that book and go play with your granddad. He wants your neat hand with a paintbrush on some new toy soldiers." At that, Granddad would call down the attic stairs, "*Miniatures*, Ella. *Models*. *Figures*. I do not play with toys."

When it wasn't Grandma sweeping James here or there, it was his mother. When she was at home. Reenie would swoop in through the Parrett house door to his bedroom to wail, "James, I'm late! Oh, baby, did you forget you had a make-up Italian lesson? Hurry up! But you can't go to Mrs. Tucci's in that T-shirt. It looks like an explosion in a fireworks factory. Here—" "Here" usually meant a white shirt, or perhaps it was the black Pittsburgh Camerata T-shirt she pulled out. As for his dad, Phil Parrett spent much of his time off at the university or holed up in his workshop. Somehow it was always when James had hoarded up a morning or afternoon to himself that his dad appeared, full of worry about not spending more time with him, to steer him off to the Natural History Museum or a concert or the

National Aviary. As if he cared about birds in cages or concerts Reenie wasn't singing in.

The summer James spent in Maine with his Parrett grandparents had been just as frustrating. Gran and Grandpa might have retired as second violin and first bassoon with the Boston Philharmonic Orchestra, but they still taught in Boston University's music department. When James wasn't out bird-watching with Grandpa or digging clams with Gran, he was in Boston suffering through music day camp while they taught their summer classes. When he gingerly suggested computer camp instead, they had stared at him as wonderingly as if he came from the planet Pluto.

Maybe he did. Or, you could say, he lived in three different countries—Black, White, and a mixed-up In-Between—even if they were all on the same planet and overlapped at the borders. The six of them worked hard at folding him into their own busy lives, but in-between was what he was. Because it made life simpler, he tried hard to say what they wanted to hear and be what they seemed to want him to be. Except musical. He never said so, but he wasn't. Well, he *could* be, but he wouldn't. He had resented music from the day at age four when he realized that it was music that took his parents away so often and for so long. Phil and Reenie didn't seem to have a clue, though, that he had been waging a war of resistance since then. They never made much fuss about the Cs and C-minuses in music classes, but then they barely noticed his As in math and English, either.

A distant sound like a slow, soft muffled rustle came whispering down to James's sharp ears, and he straightened, startled. Then he scuttled backward through the door above the well into the deeper shadow, and waited. Now and again he thought he could make out a dim musical whistle. His dream world wasn't empty after all.

The sounds, soft as dust, whispered nearer down the long, slow slope of the road, and grew into a wide, uncertain, shifting shadow as they came. Cattle. Twenty-five or thirty. Dark, gentle eyes wide, stepping neatly, their close-crowded backs moving like ripples in the moonlight, with three silent dogs for outriders, three herders at the rear. *Magical* . . . Like ghosts they slipped past, and if they saw James they showed no sign. He held his breath until they vanished into shadow farther down the slope. When they were gone, he rose to his feet and tipped his head back toward the warm night sky. He took a deep breath and felt the air . . . *sparkle* inside him. He wanted more than anything to run away up the moonlit road, but thought fearfully, *I need to go back.* He had learned to walk gingerly in his dreams and not to think too much or look too hard. He knew that if a dream place were to become familiar—if he were to remember it on waking—the gates could close against him and he might never find his way in again. Night dreams shriveled if you looked at them straight on out in the sunlight. James turned and slipped back through the door in the wall.

As he did, a cock crowed and James, as startled as if it were a warning of a dragon approaching and not the sunrise, closed and bolted the door and fled up the stairs.

three

"SIR? YOUR BREAKFAST, SIR."

James stirred awake to the smell of bacon and scrambled eggs and opened his eyes to see his father standing over him with an old-fashioned wicker breakfast-in-bed tray.

"Wha' time is it?" James raised his arm to peer at his watch. Nine o'clock!

"Mom left for the rehearsal hall half an hour ago," Phil said. "I was going to roll you out of bed when her taxi came, but she said to let you enjoy your jet lag."

James sat up and stretched his arms up over his head. "I don't think I have any. I mean, it *feels* like nine o'clock. What time is it in Pittsburgh?"

"Four a.m. But look at it this way: By Pittsburgh

time you'll be going to bed five hours early tonight, so it all evens out." He raised the tray. "Do you want your bacon and scrambled eggs here or in the kitchen? We ought to do some sightseeing to celebrate your first day, and the sooner we get out the door the better. So which'll it be?"

Back to sleep, James would have liked to say. He hadn't wanted to come to London. His parents had promised that they would have the entire summer all together for a change, at home, with maybe a visit to Grandpa and Gran Parrett in Maine. They had *promised.* And then the singer Nela Androvic was hurt in a car crash, and the group Concentus (who were famous and played original four-hundred-year-old instruments) asked Reenie to replace her on their tour of Europe. James and his dad got to go as far as London; traveling everywhere else with the group would be too expensive.

James planned to hate London.

"Here, I guess," he said in a colorless voice. "It'll be faster."

Phil put the tray down on the bed. "Good. Today'll

be fun. London has a lot to see that I've never seen myself and always wanted to. I thought we could catch a ride on one of the open-top tour buses, then start off with Madame Tussaud's Wax Museum, and after that, who knows? The Museum of London is a lot closer, but I think that'll be more interesting after you've seen something of the city. Look, I'll go tidy up in the kitchen, and when you're dressed we'll take off. Okay?"

"Okay." James agreed, but once his father was out of the room, his shoulders slumped. In tour-guide mode, his father was unstoppable. James suspected that he was either baffled or alarmed by kids in general, and worked on the principles of (a) keep it educational or (b) keep them moving so that he wouldn't lapse into a shy silence.

Twenty minutes later, showered and dressed, James picked up his socks and sneakers and followed the striding rhythm of left-hand notes and chords of Thelonious Monk's "Misterioso" to the piano in the sitting room. Phil sat on the forward edge of the bench, hunched forward, dark hair flopped down over his forehead, his left hand stomping out note, chord, note, chord, while his right danced through the melody. His eyes were half-closed, his head tilted to one side, and he wore a look both blissed-out and intent that James knew meant he was hearing the sax and bass and percussion slide in over the piano line. Glad of any delay in their attack on London, James quietly set his shoes on the floor and stretched out on the sofa. "Misterioso" was followed by "Epistrophy," so it was more than ten minutes before Phil stopped, blinked, straightened, and saw that he had an audience. The reprieve was over.

With Madame Tussaud's, lunch, the nearby London Planetarium, and the London Zoo (or about a third of it, plus a lifesaving snack in the tearoom) under their belts, James and his dad returned to the Clerkenwell apartment at six. No—"flat," not "apartment," a weary James reminded himself. The "flat"—the English word for the American "apartment"—was what his parents called it, probably because Cousin Charles did. *Whatever*, James thought vaguely, suddenly too exhausted to care. Once inside its front door, he managed a convincing, "That was great!" and even a brisk walk down the hallway to his bedroom. But there he collapsed on the bed in a Raggedy-Andy-doll sprawl. Between one deep breath and what seemed the next, half an hour passed. Even the slam of the flat's front door at his mother's return left him sleeping, and he awoke only when he heard the sound of fingernails scratching gently at his bedroom door and a voice gasping, "Help! Starving! Fo-o-o-d!"

Taking the list of restaurants and local map Cousin Charles had left for them, they walked out to Clerkenwell Road and across to follow Turnmill and Cowcross Streets down past the Underground station and up into Smithfield, where they ate at Smith's, across from the famous meat market. Afterward, full of beef and chips and salad, they walked home in the last glimmers of sunshine.

"Feeling better?" Reenie asked.

"Lots," said James. "Most expensive French fries I've ever had."

She slid him a sly grin. "You've probably earned them. Any blisters today?"

"No," James lied. He didn't look in his dad's direction. He had a small blister on the ball of one foot, but a strip of adhesive tape had taken care of it. "Can't you come with us tomorrow?"

"Can you?" Phil asked quickly. "You aren't rehearsing. We can be back in plenty of time for you to rest and eat and shift gears before we take off for Wigmore Hall and your concert. We don't need to go far. Museum of London? Tower of London?"

Reenie, walking between the two of them, gave a squeeze to their linked arms. "Sounds good, but they've set up a BBC radio interview for the consort and me for mid-morning, and Erewhon Records is going to take us to lunch at the Savoy—with Gianni Ricci. Can you believe it? Gianni Ricci!"

Phil grinned. "Are you going to squeal and ask for an autograph?"

He sounded as if it didn't matter whether Reenie came with them or not. As if all that mattered was the concert. Musicians! *Music*. This summer was already like every other summer, James thought bitterly. Every other year. He might as well check the telephone book for the nearest library as soon as they got back to the apartm—the *flat*. At home, after his friend Tyrone moved to St. Louis, the Carnegie Library was all that saved James from being packed off to the nearest set of musical cousins every time both his parents and grandparents had to be out for the day. Now was the time to make "I'll be okay" plans for London. It was only a matter of days before his dad would get antsy about being chief tour guide and start drumming his fingers on everything from tables and walls to his chin or knees. That meant he was itching to get his hands on a piano, or get back to working on his book about a collection of old musical instrument makers who'd been dead for four hundred years. James gave him two or three more days. Five, tops.

Reenie's concert at Wigmore Hall earned enthusiastic reviews in the London *Times* and *Telegraph* and *Independent*, and on Thursday she and Concentus traveled north to Manchester and from there were to go on to Edinburgh. Phil's tour-guide enthusiasm wavered on Saturday, the third day he and James were on their own, when he took the afternoon off to go to the British Library and look up something or other about one of his long-dead lute or guitar makers. James had gone with him earlier in the day to look for presents for each of his grandparents—beginning with a military miniature Granddad Hackaday didn't have. They found a great shop named *Under Two Flags*, but a few minutes earlier James had felt a sudden shiver or tingle that left him feeling strange. When faced with choosing between a brightly painted Zulu warrior from the Battle of Isandlwana, or a far more beautifully modeled but unpainted one in kit form for half again as much, he hadn't been able to make up his mind. He decided he would go again after lunch, on his own, but it had been a long, foot-blistering three-and-a-half days, and he made the mistake of stretching out on his bed "for five minutes."

His bedroom in the flat wasn't so bad, really. The soft-green and ivory striped wallpaper was quiet enough, and James decided that he liked the cheerful old framed prints on the walls of pop-eyed birds and stiff-legged animals. The bed was harder than his own, but he was yawning as he smiled at a loopy-looking lion and promptly toppled into a deep, dreamless sleep.

Much to James's relief after three days of his father's cooking, Phil treated him to pizza with sausage at Beppi's in Exmouth Market, a short walk away. On the way back to Cousin Charles's, his dad looked down at him with a vaguely puzzled frown. "James, isn't there anything you'd like to do tomorrow? Um . . . tennis? I saw in the paper this morning that Wimbledon's started. I suppose tickets are hard to come by, but we could try."

James shrugged. "I don't care. Whatever you'd like to do."

"I'll take that as a no, then . . ." His dad looked about to say something more, but settled for a helpless shrug, and didn't.

The rest of the evening was a performance on television of the opera *The Magic Flute*. James enjoyed the first part—the bits with Papageno the birdcatcher—in spite of himself, but after the first act his eyelids drooped, and he slid lower and lower on the sofa until in the second act he almost slid off. Phil sighed and sent him to bed.

In the middle of the night James drifted up into a dream, but it was of Grandpa Parrett stalking through the Maine woods with the long-legged, stiffly swooping gait of a heron, which was strange because Grandpa was shortish and stout. A stream rippled and splashed over stones nearby, but oddly, it sounded as if it were far off, and more like water running from a tap . . .

The dream again.

James felt himself throw off the sheet and sit up eagerly. He knew where he was and where he was going, and he saw that his watch read 2:30. This time his feet groped for his sneakers and slipped into them without being told to. He thought dreamily, *Better tie them,* but when he looked down, his fingers were already pulling the bows in the laces tight. *Go through the sitting room,* he told himself. *They squeak on the kitchen flooring.*

Silence. Door. Stairs. Water running. Hallway. Door. He pulled the cord for the basement light, and the basement was just as it was before, except that this time the ceiling light was brighter and didn't blink out. The upended tea chest stood just where he had left it, but in the brighter light the shimmer in front of it was much harder to see. James reached out to the light cord and gave it a tug—*that's better!*—then felt his way down the steps in darkness. Moving like a sleepwalker, he crossed the floor to the window that waited in the air, shifted the tea chest an inch or two to the right, and climbed out onto the same moonlit stair.

The same and not the same. Now the bare tree-tops that fringed the sky above the upper stair were in full leaf, and they danced in a summer-warm breeze. The heavy oaken door at the bottom of the stairs opened onto the same well basin and the same three houses across the road, but now the bright moon shared the sky with pale-edged clouds and the dipping, soaring song of a bird.

Except for the bird's song and the splashing water, the world was still silent. The air was clear and sweet, and as James took a deep breath of it, all his senses seemed to tingle.

He reached down behind him for the bucket and, when he stepped down toward the well, pulled it forward to serve as a doorstop. One step down brought him to a wider step at the water's edge, and from that he gained the stone rim at the side of the well. Jumping down into the road, he crossed it to take a look back at the place he had come from. As he went, he felt hard earth underfoot at the verge, and in the road, soft dust in what he supposed were wheel ruts. Looking back where he had come from, he could see three different rooflines atop the wall along the lane. Except for two little windows high under the middle roofline, the door above the well was the only opening. The well itself stood at the corner of its wall, at a wide place where two roadways met and crossed. Past the house where he stood, the cross lane dipped down and ran away tamely between hedges and fields. Beyond the wide crossing, James's own road dipped gently down between shadowy houses and garden walls toward a jumble of shadows. The jumble might have been a town sleeping under a cloud in the night sky, or a sea of trees, or both together.

Curiosity plucked at him, but houses and people were not what he wanted. He turned his back on them and considered the road uphill. Beyond the buildings on the well's side of the road, the wall continued as a high garden wall along a gentle upward slope. The moon was lower in the sky than it had been the first time, and the black moon shadows were longer, but the road was still a tempting silver-gray ribbon. It unrolled in gentle dips and climbs up to a tree-fringed crest and then on into the hilly distance.

Follow the yellow dust road, James thought, and felt almost lifted off his feet by a rush of silliness. He gave a leap in the air and then, overcome by freedom, turned four cartwheels in a row up the lane. In the waking world he would have tightened up and crashed after the first or second. Elated, he shook himself like a wet puppy. Eyes, ears, nose—all were more awake than he had known they could be.

James stood breathless in the road and waited for the dream to carry him along with it, but nothing happened—except that the bird sang on somewhere out in the fields. It sang unwearied, each clear lift and fall of notes like liquid silver, each unlike the last, each a mingling of mourning and joy. James had never heard any bird so magical. Its slow, rising *piu, piu, piu, piu!* drew him up the road, reeling him in on a silver cord. Spellbound, he padded softly along between the high garden wall on his right and moon-pale fields on the left in an enchanted world that seemed empty of any other life. He slowed when he came to the place where the wall turned away from the road. The song came from close by in the hedge that followed the road upward, but as James drew near, it broke off. With a soft *tuc*, a quick, harsh little *kerr!* and a faint flutter in the hedge, the mysterious bird darted up and away. Some of James's giddiness fled with it. Being in his own private world, being his own self and no one else's, felt delicious but a little sad, and the thought that it was after all only a dream had followed him like a shadow.

But then he brushed the shadow away and set off again uphill.

As the road climbed, the whiffs of cow from down near the houses faded, but in the hedge-fenced fields small shakes of head and twitches of tail turned shadows into the horses he scented. Farther along he passed a gate on the left, and beyond it open heath and patches of grassland stretched away and overhill.

A few yards past the gate, James's heart gave a sudden skip of alarm, and he wheeled to give the gate a sharp look. Had he, for a flicker of a moment, seen something move by the bushes behind it?

Perhaps not, but he went on more cautiously.

The road itself ran upward between an earthen embankment on the left and the hedge on the right on its way to the first, low crest. Beyond that point, it dipped down among fields and patches of woods before climbing again. James turned aside at a gate on the right and clambered over the stile beside it. A few yards up through the tussocky grass a grove of sturdy trees stood dark against the sky, and he found a wide, clear view of the world he had dreamed himself into.

In the moonlight it was as unreal as it was beautiful. Night insects sang their creaky songs, and somewhere in the fields the notes of the mysterious bird rose up again. The grass whispered, and the leaves above stirred and sighed. Far below, James could see that the high wall uphill from his well enclosed an orchard and neglected gardens. Down past the buildings that sheltered the well, he could see moon-silvered gardens, church steeples, trees, and rooftops sprawling downward, huddling closer and closer along crooked streets and lanes until the rooftops crowded out the gardens and the trees. A huge building, long, with graceful pinnacles at the roof peak on each end and a tall, square-topped tower in its middle, stood atop a low rise at the center of that great hive of rooftops. Far off to the left, where the sky was paler, the bright silver of a broadening stream wandered out toward the horizon. Once or twice a distant bark challenged the silence of the sleeping town, and once a mournful answering howl. It was on the heels of the howl that James heard a stranger sound. As it drew nearer, he knew it for the whisper of feet on the dusty road, and he shrank back against the tree trunk.

The people who came striding over the crest of the hill and down toward the town this time were no cattle herders. James counted thirty before they had all swept past, men and women, girls and boys, and tiny children. Handsome, hard-faced and intent, dressed in fantastic garments—some so ragged that they looked like festoons of lace—they moved like wraiths, with no sound but the dusty rustle of bare feet. The tall, hawk-nosed man who led them swept the heath on either side with a wary eye, but few of the others looked aside. James, in puzzled fascination, watched them, wild and eerie, swoop away down the road.

What did it mean?

Perhaps the dream meant for him to follow them away toward adventure. But that thought fled almost as soon as it had come. A sense of menace—and the strong, sour smell of unwashed bodies—lingered in their wake. James watched until they reached and passed his wall and the well. Just beyond, they divided and vanished into the streets and lanes that led down toward the town.

James drew a long breath in relief, and sat down with his back against the tree trunk. It was good to have the world empty again and not to feel that the dream was going to sweep him off against his will after all. Leave that to his dad, Tour Guide Extraordinary. Or his mom, who made friends just by liking everyone and shining her 400-watt smile at them—and who honestly could not understand why James should try to keep himself so much to himself. He suspected that during Christmas and summer vacations she probably shooed him off to lessons in this or that, or computer day camp, or the classes at the City Music Center as much in hopes that he might make a friend or two as learn anything. At least she had finally stopped asking why he never had Albert or Chaz or Denzel, friends from his old elementary school, over anymore. He could hardly tell her it was jealousy, that he couldn't stand going to *their* houses. All three had parents who left their work behind in their offices or stores and were home by six o'clock, who ate dinner and watched TV and went to movies together, and who took ordinary family vacations to Disney World or Washington, D.C., or Williamsburg, Virginia. James in the end had grown so jealous that he hated them for it. He had pushed them away and still felt ashamed that in third grade he had once literally pushed Albert down his own front porch steps—*hard*—and called him "Marshmallow-Pie Face." It wasn't because Albert was overweight (though he was) or that he was white (the really pale kind that went pink after just ten minutes in the sun) but because his plain, plump mother with the wild, wispy hair made the world's best chocolate pecan cookies, and could play computer games well enough to win, and actually listened all the way through to their excited, scene-by-scene accounts of any movie they had just come back from. *All the way through.*

James felt even guiltier because Albert, who was a fiendish collector of military badges and buttons, must still miss their visits to Granddad's attic rooms with their display tables covered with Civil War landscape models for the siege of Port Hudson and the attack on Fort Wagner. James didn't care about the names of the officers or the patterns of shifting armies, but when the three of them acted out the battles with the tiny soldiers, he did love to watch Granddad move his troops. His arthritis-knobby, trembly black fingers knew the strategy of every charge and sortie. He always took the black Union troops when they were in an action, and made the boys move the Rebels. When they argued it was time to trade, he never would. "My battlefields, my rules," was his answer, and he repeated it calmly until one day they gave up. Now there was a big table with a layout of the Battle of Gettysburg, and another of a skirmish of the Red River War of 1874, between the Ninth and Tenth U.S. Cavalry Regiments—the black Buffalo Soldiers—and the Kiowas.

James hadn't really tried to make friends after he changed schools. For the past year he had drawn even further into himself. His parents couldn't guess why, and he didn't want to say, even though they might have let him off the hook with the after-school music classes. The truth was that of all the boys in his classes or in Granddad's Bethel Youth Choir, his voice was the only one that hadn't changed. It was still a high, little-boy treble, and the only reason he didn't have to sit and sing with the girls was that he faked it. He moved his mouth, but made no sound. If anyone had caught on, they hadn't said so. The odd thing was that he couldn't help *listening*. Fiercely. When next to him Anneke Wallis slid—and she often did—off her note by even the finest hair's breadth, it gave him shudders down in the very center of himself, as if she were a piece of chalk scritching up a blackboard. It was a mystery to him why he cared. He stared out over this new, silent world, and wondered.

Afterward, it was an even greater mystery to him why he did what he did. The clear, magical notes of the last song Reenie had sung at Wigmore Hall on Wednesday night were suddenly as alive in his mind as if she were standing close behind him. And with that glorious voice in his mind, he joined in and sang into the night air. . . .

> *All the night my sleeps are full of dreams,*
> *My eyes are full of streams.*
> *My heart takes no delight*
> *To see the fruits and joys that some do find*
> *And mark the storms are me assigned . . .*

As the last clear note blew away, and before James could take a breath for the next verse, an uncanny moment's silence fell. Not even a cricket chirruped until, like a clap of thunder all around him, trees and hedges, sky and scrub and grass exploded in sound. James leaped up in astonished fright and clapped his hands over his ears. After the first stunned moment, he dropped them in wonder.

Birds. *Birds!* Thousands—hundreds of thousands. Millions? It was as if every songbird in the world had flocked together and in one staggering moment puffed up small chests, opened throats, and shouted small hearts up into the sky to burst in red and silver showers.

Once James had caught his breath and looked out and away, he understood.

The sky had paled to a pearly gray, and far off to the left—to the east—the wisps of cloud on the horizon blushed the color of apricots, with a thin line of gold brushed along their bottoms. The birds' great song, still ringing, was their welcome to the dawn. James felt a little foolish—it was, after all, only a dream—but like an awkward Cinderella dashing to catch the pumpkin coach at the stroke of twelve, he hitched up his pajama bottoms and ran.

four

REENIE RETURNED ON SUNDAY, BUT FOR THE next three days was kept so busy with rehearsals and the master classes Concentus gave for music students, that Phil's sightseeing campaign continued. On the Wednesday of the Everlasting Tour, Phil raised an arm and waved his guide book as James fell behind on their way out of the Tower of London. "James! Come along. If we take the Underground straight along to the South Bank from here, we can get a bite to eat before we head for the Eye at two."

James sighed as he snapped the camera case shut and handed it over. The thought of the London Eye, a five-hundred-foot-high Ferris wheel, made his stomach lurch even from miles away. Seven days, and his father was still going at being a tourist in the way that, once or twice a year, he attacked a new workshop project: drawing detailed plans for the new mandolin or pandora, visiting every hardwood supplier in the tri-state area, sometimes going even farther afield to find the perfect pieces of cherry and ebony and bow wood. Next he vanished into his workroom, cutting, shaping, joining, then rubbing away in endless hours of finishing. He paused from time to time—when he remembered—to go off and teach a class at the university, or eat a meal, or snatch a few hours' sleep, but it was like a terrible head cold. There wasn't a cure. It had to run its course.

The thought of another long day stretching on before him left James feeling as desperate as he was confused. He was going to be yawning himself to death on one of the last concert-free evenings Reenie would have at home with them before she and the five members (violin, bass viol, pandora, lute, and flute) of Concentus took off on the next leg of their tour. Great. He longed to have it be August already.

Or better still, he realized with a start, to be back at Cousin Charles's flat and alone. He had begun to have a niggling sense—a prickle at the back of his mind—of something he wanted to remember. Something. A dream.

He wanted to remember the dream.

To James's surprise, when he and his dad reached Tower Hill Underground station, Phil actually noticed that something was wrong. He cocked his head to one side and said, "You feel okay? You look a little green around the edges."

"I'm fine."

His dad frowned. "It could be a summer cold coming on. Maybe we'd better go back to the flat. You can sack out, and I'll go look for a pharmacy and get us some vitamin C and whatnot."

At the flat a rummage in Cousin Charles's medicine cabinet produced a fever thermometer. When James's temperature proved normal, Phil dithered for a moment and then decided that he would go in search of vitamin C anyway, just to be safe.

Another afternoon free! James was so relieved to be off his feet that he kicked off his shoes and stretched out on the bed, hands behind his head, but not to rest. Even if it meant he could never revisit it, he wanted to find a thread of the dream, enough to pull and unravel. . . .

He fell asleep.

When he awoke at three, he remembered the shimmer. And the stairs. And the moonlit world.

It had seemed so *real*.

James lay on the bed and stared at the green and ivory wallpaper stripes without seeing them. So? Some dreams *were* alarmingly real, and it *had* been a dream. If he had been awake, he would have remembered it all along, wouldn't he? It was dreams you forgot. Even thinking about its being real was crazy.

Too bad. They had been great dreams.

James's mind skittered away from giving a name to the whatsis-in-the-basement, a shyness that was pretty silly considering that the whatsis wasn't real. In the dream, thinking of the mysterious circle as "the shimmer" was just a way of evading the question of what it was. A "door"? A "window"? He might as well have backed even further away and called it "an opening." "Portal" would sound geekishly Star Trekky.

Parallel universe stuff. Alternate realities. *Seriously* geeky. Besides, time gates, magic mirrors, star gates, black holes—all of those things—might present a sort of doorway or opening when you came at them head-on, but the whatsis was a . . . a *thing* with both a front and a back in the here and now. With nothing at all in between . . . and yet with a whole world in between. How had his brain ever come up with that one?

James took a deep breath and decided that what he ought to do was pull the pillow over his head and go back to sleep, but "ought to" lost out to "had to." He was going to have to go downstairs and open the basement door, or . . . or explode. He swung his legs to the floor, pulled on his sneakers, checked the pocket of his shorts for his keys to the flat, and went—more slowly with each flight of stairs—down to the ground floor hallway. When he reached the basement door and turned the handle, his stomach gave a small, unpleasant hiccup, and he realized that his heart was *tick-tock-tick*ing like a metronome set at its fastest pace.

He didn't see anything at first because his eyes had not adjusted to the darkness, but he knew, as soon as he pulled the light cord and saw the tea chest, the boiler, the sink, and the tea chests stacked in the corner, what else he was going to see. The shimmer was so transparent that for a moment he thought, *I'm just imagining it because I want it to be there*, but when he turned the light off and closed his eyes while he counted to twenty, there it was when he opened them again. He could see the stone wall and the shadowy stair through the shimmer.

It was really, truly, actually there.

James retreated up the steps, closed the door gently, and fled up the four flights of stairs two steps at a time.

The next night was Reenie's last before leaving for Germany. Dinner was chicken Tetrazzini, peas, and carrot soufflé from Cousin Charles's dwindling freezer supply, and James was silent from first bite to last, not that Phil or Reenie noticed. His parents, in fact, would have blinked and brought out the fever thermometer again if he suddenly turned into the chatterbox he desperately longed to be. It would be a huge relief to be able to tell about the dreams and have them exclaim, "How odd!" and have them laugh away the crazy idea that any of it could be real, that Cousin Charles could just happen to have a time portal in the basement.

While they cleared their plates away to the kitchen and Reenie struggled to cut slices from a still half-frozen chocolate cream cake, the talk turned to the details of the tour schedule that was going to take Shareen Parrett and Concentus across Europe from Frankfurt, to Prague, Milan, and Barcelona, returning to London for a week before taking off again to Munich, Köln, and Stockholm, and finishing up in St. Petersburg on the twenty-second of July.

"It's a tough schedule," Phil observed, "but a great finale. I'm jealous. I've never seen St. Petersburg. Maybe James and I should fly out to join you for those two days. What do you say, James?"

James blinked and looked up from his cake with a flicker of real interest. "To *Russia*? Sure!" Then, as his parents settled down to making plans, he went back to puzzling over the feeling of unease that had made him wish he hadn't taken a second helping of chocolate cake. But he suspected it wasn't really the cake. He tried hard to concentrate on the big flat-screen TV—they were in the sitting room, watching a DVD of *A.I.*—but he kept losing track of the story. Images of the silent hillside and the sleeping town, of unpaved roads, dark houses, and shadowy streets crept up on him and filled his imagination, crowding out the sad adventures of the robot child.

He slipped out to the kitchen to pour himself a glass of milk and went back to try again. He *wanted* to know what happened to the robot kid Haley Joel Osment was playing in the movie, but all he could think of was the dream that wasn't a dream.

Now he knew it was real.

But not what to do about it.

"Your mom's sleeping in," Phil said the next morning, "but you and I can take off to the Safeway and do some grocery shopping as soon as we've had our breakfast. We should be able to catch a cab back from the Barbican Centre and be in plenty of time to take Mom to meet the rest of the group at noon. Their plane doesn't leave until three-thirty." He rummaged in the refrigerator. "There's no milk or cereal left, but there is butter and honey. It's not exactly summerish, but what would you say to a wicked stack of pancakes?"

"Okay, sure," James said. Anything that would keep him too busy to dither "Will I? Won't I?" was welcome. None of his old fantasies of having a world to himself were any help now that he actually could *have* one. . . .

The pancakes, made from scratch, were a little rubbery, but double butter and honey made up for that, and the grocery expedition was—accidentally—a great success. On their way along Clerkenwell Road, they passed a stretch where the old buildings of shops, studios, and workshops now seemed mostly to have been converted to fashionable "loft living" above the shop level. But there were a few holdouts. Beside a still-shabby door between an elderly snack bar and a shoe repair shop, Phil caught sight of a handsome oval sign: *Euan & Gillian January, Lutemakers, Second Floor.* He stopped, looked up at the windows above, wavered, and went on. His feet didn't exactly drag, but James could feel him yearning backward. Phil himself had once made a beautiful six-course lute, but he had never been satisfied with its tone. For a year he had been talking about trying again, perhaps making a ten- or twelve-course version.

"Let's go back," James said quickly. He was unwilling to pass up such a perfect chance to slow down or even stop the Let's-Not-Miss-Anything Tour of London. With luck he might win the time he needed to . . . to decide what to do.

Phil wavered. "It's all right. I can stop by anytime. I—" He turned. "James?"

James was already on his way back. By the time his dad arrived at the front door, he had reached the top of the first worn wooden flight of stairs. He was waiting above at the workshop door with its beautifully lettered sign, *January • Lutes, Vihuelas, & Baroque Guitars*, when his father caught up.

"I'll just introduce myself, and come back another time," Phil said apologetically as he knocked on the door. "I thought after lunch we might take the Tube down to Blackfriars and walk across the river to take a look at the big Tate Modern gallery and the Globe Theatre."

James gave an automatic smile. "Why not?"

They came away with an invitation from the Januarys to Phil to return the following morning for a tour of the workshop and a demonstration of some of their special equipment. With that settled, the groceries bought, and Concentus waved off to the airport, James was perfectly happy to set off after lunch for the Tube station, Blackfriars, and the River Thames. Trudging around an art gallery in a cavernous former power station was a small price to pay when it could well be the last Parrett Tour of the summer. The lute-making Januarys had lost their assistant in May, and James could almost see the wheels turning in his father's head. He wouldn't be able to resist volunteering to step in "just part-time" for the next three weeks, and James knew what "just part-time" meant.

After the gallery and the Globe Theatre, James and Phil lingered on the Millennium Footbridge over the River Thames to take photos. James was taking a turn as photographer when suddenly he lowered the camera, turned, and blinked furiously. Hanging in the air in front of him, three feet above the gleaming metal grid of the walkway underfoot, was a faint, almost invisible shadow in the shape of a wide oval. The bridge was in full sunshine, but James had not seen the shape until the moment before he walked through it and at its faint fizz jerked as if he had been stung. He looked around him. No one else appeared to notice a thing. With hundreds of sightseers crossing the river on the broad walkway, scores of them must have walked right through it, just as he had. James retraced his steps, but there was nothing to be seen, and he decided that it must have been the dazzle of sunshine on the camera lens, or in his head. It came from thinking so much about what he had or might have seen, what was or might not be in the Clerkenwell Close basement. Uncertain what to do, James stood stock-still, two-thirds of the way across the gleaming arch over the river while the press of tourists and Londoners on a day out poured past him like water around a dark rock.

Almost all white water. One black family, mother holding a six-year-old's hand, father pushing a toddler's stroller. A swirl of Japanese teenagers. Here and there faces coffee-brown like James's, but mostly Indian or Pakistani, with born-in-London accents.

"Did you get it?" his dad called.

Phil, in chinos and rolled-up shirtsleeves, stood about twenty feet farther along the bridge. His ancient backpack sagged under the weight of three new art books, the largest a volume on music and musicians in twentieth-century art.

"No," James called back to his father. His knees felt not exactly wobbly, but for a moment reluctant to work. "My finger slipped before I got the focus set," he said. "I'll take another one."

"Be sure to get St. Paul's in too."

As James stepped farther to the left, camera to his eye, the flow of people coming toward him and most of those coming from the South Bank theatre and gallery at his back parted good-humoredly to keep from crossing in front of him. The moment his view was clear, he pressed the button.

"Got it!"

Mr. Parrett moved across to the downstream-side railing and leaned there to try for another look back toward the Globe Theatre on the South Bank, but he was too far over the brow of the bridge to see it again. James reached into his pocket for the camera's lens cap as he moved to follow, but stopped suddenly and turned. While he was concentrating on the camera's viewfinder, he had forgotten the vanished shimmer.

"Sorry," he blurted to a girl who had to hop aside to keep from stumbling against him. Another step brought him to what he thought was the spot where he had stood. Nothing. He shifted back and forth to try to catch sight of any shift of light, but caught only the mildly curious stares of passersby. At least he wasn't the only one standing still over the middle of the river. Some took photos. Others simply stood. One man, shirtless, in bicycle shorts and helmet, held one arm up in salute to something. The beautiful bridge? The sunny day? The bright City so vivid between the river and the sky that it looked as if you could reach out and touch it? The colorful sweep of the crowds off the bridge and up the wide way of St. Paul's Hill to the great cathedral made a scene too crisply perfect to be real. More than anything, it looked like a computer-generated scene out of a fantasy film.

James turned back to keep looking for the shimmer. Because he didn't want to look like a total nerfball, stretching and stooping to look for something that wasn't there, he raised the camera to use the viewfinder and its zoom as a spyglass. If his father turned around, he'd be happy to see James interested enough to be snapping photos.

James pulled the scene in front of him closer with the zoom and began to scan the space ten to fifteen feet ahead of him as the walkers passed through it. He held his breath and concentrated on moving the camera slowly enough to catch anything that might be there. Nothing. He moved forward.

He was about to give up when the viewfinder darkened. In the same moment that he felt his face tingle he heard a child shriek, almost in his ear, and his finger twitched on the button, snapping a photo when he did not mean to, of a scene he did not believe he was seeing. As he jerked back, someone moving too quickly to stop slammed against his shoulder. The camera went flying in one direction, James stumbling in the other. The child shrieked again.

"Daddy, look! That boy! He's—"

five

THE SHOCK OF ICY WATER DROVE THE BREATH from James's lungs. His throat closed, and he sank, stunned by the impact of the fall. His mind was blank, his eyes dark. Then, suddenly, painfully, his head was jerked upward as a hand hauled him up into the air by his hair.

"Curses! His hair's too short," a voice gasped. Another hand grasped the neck of his shirt.

"Hold fast!" a sharp voice commanded. "You, waterman, catch his arm. Where in Creation did he come from?"

"I didn't see, sir. Not a thing 'til we heard the splash."

The two men struggled to haul the boy into the

boat. The third man, older and stout, leaned his weight to the other side to balance them.

"Bless us, 'tis only a lad!" the first man exclaimed breathlessly as he hauled away with one hand. With the other he caught at his velvet hat with the green ostrich plume as it was about to blow into the water.

"And a blackamoor at that," the waterman wheezed as he heaved the boy over the gunwale.

The third man sniffed as he settled back into his cushioned seat. "Yes, yes, a strange fish, but get to your oars, man! I'm late enough as 'tis for reaching St. Albans before supper."

The waterman obligingly pulled away strongly at his oars as the first man, sitting in the second passenger seat, cradled James between his knees and spread his woolen cloak over him.

"The lad's half naked," he marveled. "And his feet are unshod. In weather like this!"

"I've seen the like before," the waterman said, and he hurried the pace of his oars. "With poor souls who jump in from the bridge. The tide when it's running up between them bridge feet is fearsome. Peels clean off their clothes and shoes, like skinning eels."

"From the bridge?" The stout man snorted. "And be carried this far upriver in near-freezing water? He would be long dead."

As he spoke, the boat bumped against the palings of a wharf, and at the waterman's call men huddled around a fire in a brazier moved quickly. Hands reached down to help. James, limp as a drowned cat, heard nothing. The first he knew, he was being swept along at a trot between the waterman and the man with the green plume up a street of tall houses with tile fronts and richly carved doorways, windows, and eaves. Dazed, he saw the wide windows glitter in a pale winter sunlight that dazzled his eyes. He could not stop shuddering with the cold. Then the men were turning in at a plainer door under the hanging sign of a stern-faced man wearing a halo that looked like a gold dinner plate.

Why a church? James wondered weakly as the light dimmed. *Am I dead? Why are they all in costume?*

Inside, the mingled smells of tobacco, beer, and warm bodies, and the hubbub of talk and laughter told him *No, not dead.* A fire burned brightly in a wide stone fireplace, and men with pipes and tankards turned to stare. One, a lean, red-cheeked toothpick of a man, rose so that the men could set James in his place near the fire on one of the inglenook benches.

The waterman held his callused hands out to the fire and cocked an eye at Plumed Hat. "I don't grudge to help, but I must pay a ha'penny to the lad who's watched my boat," he said.

Plumed Hat frowned as he fingered the purse that hung at his belt, then pulled out a coin. With a nod of thanks, the waterman shouldered his way through the knot of curious drinkers come to stare, and out the door.

Plumed Hat, who was a blue-eyed, middling-young man with long, curling dark hair, waved his hat in the air and shouted, "Potboy! Mulled ale and a cup of hot rumney!" Then he stood James up on unsteady feet to wrap the cloak more tightly around him, and set him back down on the bench.

"Why, 'tis an African!" one voice exclaimed.

"And wet as a spaniel," said another as James's wet

shorts and T-shirt dripped down his legs and onto the hearth. "Did ye fish him from the river?"

At Plumed Hat's nod, a third voice announced importantly, "He'll be from the trader that tied up at St. Katherine's dock this Wednesday past, come from Africa with a cargo of ivory and fine woods, and the like. It's anchored in the Pool now, beside the *Dragon*, that's been fitted up for the Indies. You'll see—this lad will have fallen in and washed upriver with the tide."

Another shook his head. "And come under the bridge without a battering? 'Tis a fearsome current, and to ride through't is to thread a needle in a storm."

The potboy came pushing his way through with a tankard and a small beaker held high, and the men shifted place, then stepped back again as the door opened. The newcomer was the stout passenger from the boat, who, after a look around, moved to a stool in the window corner and beckoned to the potboy.

"Boy! Mulled clary!" he snapped, and arranged himself on the stool with his back against the wall. "The lad. He's alive still, I see?"

Plumed Hat looked up from holding the beaker

for James to drink and grinned. "Alive, but still a-shake as a sail in a crosswind."

"Boy!" the stout gentleman barked. "D'ye speak English? If ye do, speak up! Where'd you fall in the river?"

James blinked and looked muzzily around the ring of strange faces. "Fr-from the bridge?" he whispered hoarsely.

"Ah. And where d'ye live, lad?"

James felt a stab of alarm. Who were these people? What had happened to him? Why were they asking these questions? "In Clerkenwell?" he answered cautiously.

Plumed Hat looked interested. "Where in Clerkenwell?"

"By the w-well?" James faltered.

One of the men nodded wisely. "The old nunnery. My Lord Newcastle and some others have pulled down half of the priory lodgings. I warrant they'll be building great houses in their places. They have many workers and craftsmen, Flemish and Italians among 'em. Africans, too, it would seem."

"And who is to see the boy safe to Clerkenwell?" the stout man asked gruffly. "And find him shoes and trews so he does not turn icicle on the way? My coachman knows little of the town—no more do I—and I mean to be in St. Albans in good time for my supper."

James, drowsing in the fire's warmth, was startled awake when a stubble-chinned man sidled close to reach out and touch a curious finger to his cheek. "I never did thee an African near-to before," he lisped with a rotten-toothed smile.

James shrank away a little from the man's foul breath and tried to listen to Plumed Hat and the others.

"Come, St. Albans is no more than twenty miles," Plumed Hat was saying. "I can fetch the boy shoes and warm clothing ten minutes from here, and ten back. If you're bound for St. Albans, you'll go by way of Aldersgate Street. If you will be good enough to carry us so far as Beech Street, I'll walk with him from there. 'Twill do him good to warm his blood."

It was agreed, and Plumed Hat went off once James had drunk the last of his hot rumney. Whatever hot rumney was, it left a warm glow in his middle, but it made his head swim too, when it was already dazed. It could not fasten on anything—how he had come to be in the water, why the sudden cold, where he was, or who the stout man might be.

The stout gentleman had moved from his seat by the window to sit beside the drowsing boy, drinking, and putting out a hand now and again to keep him from toppling off his bench. Most of the men went back to their drinks or arguments or songs, but a handful pulled up stools, fascinated by the boy's foreignness.

"Africa! 'Tis monstrous hot there, they say," offered a small fellow with a nearsighted, peering squint. "For that, I'd not mind being there, wintertimes."

Another shook his gray locks and spat into the fire. "Not I! I've no mind to be dinner for a lion or'n elyphaunt."

"They do say there be anthropophagi there. Men who eat men," put in another. "And cockatrices and spinxes."

"And there's the one-legged folk with a foot so big 'tis said they lie on their backs and use 'em for shade from the sun."

"Nonsense!" exploded the stout gentleman. "Foolish tales repeated by travelers who fare out no farther than Tilbury docks. 'Tis a land of countries of men, and elephants do not eat 'em."

"Aye," agreed the stocky man in a rust-colored doublet and striped trunk hose who sat on the inglenook bench across the hearth from James's. "For did ye not see the great black prince riding up the river on one of the queen's own barges to visit the queen, not three months past? 'Twas a brave sight, with his plumes and particolored robes and gold collar and armlets, and his company in their finery."

James roused a little, but his head ached and he could make no sense of anything he heard, so he gave up trying, and dozed off with his head against the stout gentleman's arm. When Plumed Hat returned, he was fast asleep.

Plumed Hat carried a bundle under one arm and a pair of shoes under the other, and the men moved back to give him space by the hearth. He took off his gloves and warmed his hands and his backside for a moment at the fire before gently standing the boy on his feet and unwinding him from his cloak. James obediently sat and stood as Plumed Hat pulled on long woolen hose and a long-sleeved woolen shirt, breeches that ended just below the knee, fastened with laces and eyeholes, and a doublet with padded sleeves that was belted at the waist. As the shoes and then a knee-length cloak went on, the stout gentleman stood and stumped off toward the door.

"Come along," he ordered impatiently as Plumed Hat took James's shoulders and steered him out ahead of him. "Come along. And tell John Coachman where he must put you down."

The coach was a boxy affair with two horses, a coachman, a door on one side, and two wooden benches inside, with cushions to sit on, and lap robes. With the three of them it was crammed full, knee to knee.

"There, now," the stout gentleman said as they lurched off up the hill. "What's your name, lad?"

"James Parrett," James said without thinking.

"Parrett? An English name. 'Tis your mother who is the African, then?"

James shook his head muzzily, a shake that could

have been either a "yes" or a "no." The questions made him nervous, though he was not sure why. He wished he had not given them his name. The bitterly cold air had awakened him to the wild strangeness of his surroundings. On his side the coach had no door, only a window closed by a leather curtain rigged so that only a narrow slit was left open. Through it, James peered out at a wintry town with no cars or trucks, only horsemen, horse-drawn carts, and once in a while a coach. Figures bundled up against the cold hurried along the streets like extras in a costume movie—only, like the men in the tavern, grubbier and probably smellier.

It would have been fascinating . . .

If he hadn't known he was awake.

six

THE COACH RUMBLED PAST HIGH HOUSES with peaked roofs crowded up against a towering church and a square tower taller still. Far too large to be a parish church. A cathedral? If this was London, it was not Westminster Abbey, which James and his dad had seen from their tour bus the day before, or St. Paul's with its great dome. So where was he? His mind skittered away from the more alarming question of *When is this?* His head began to spin again, until he realized that he was holding his breath. Feeling the two men's eyes upon him, he let it out slowly and began quietly to take deep breaths of the sharp air with its tang of wood smoke. Strangely enough, with the cold air, the last trembly shivers that had quivered deep inside him even in front of the tavern fire grew fainter. By the time the coach trundled through a great stone gatehouse set in the City wall, he felt almost warm, but his confusion deepened with every minute that passed. A walled city? London? James's confusion made his head swim.

Plumed Hat kept his eye on the slit of window in the door as the coach rolled northward along a wide street lined with large houses. Removing his hat, he unhooked the leather curtain and craned out to see ahead. After a moment he called out to the coachman, "Long Lane's just ahead. Put us down just there, by the tenement on the corner."

When James and his rescuer had made their thanks and stepped down into the road, the stout gentleman looked out the window, but only to nod and to call to John Coachman to hurry on.

Plumed Hat took James by the elbow to steer him around the corner into the lane. "Come, step alive. Warm your blood."

They went on for a while at a half trot, and to James, as unsteady as he was, Long Lane *was* long. It, too, was lined with tall houses with tile fronts on the ground floors, plaster above, and tile roofs. Both the tall single-family houses on the right and the larger four- or five-family dwellings on the left had corner posts, doorposts, and lintels of richly carved oak. In each, a passageway led through the front into a court-yard where stairs climbed to the upper levels. Here and there an aproned servant hurried in or out, a child wailed, or a lean cat rubbed against a doorpost.

Apartment houses, James thought wonderingly as he panted along. Above and beyond the housetops, crowded close, was the squat tower of a church.

Plumed Hat saw James's head crane back to see. "You've not been this way before? 'Tis new built over with tenements for rich cattle brokers and tipplers."

"Tipplers?"

Plumed Hat grinned down at him. "Tavernkeepers. A good number of the houses around Smithfield are taverns, and not a few of the others are brewhouses, but you will know that."

Why would he think I know that? James thought in panic.

Smithfield . . . Where he and Phil and Reenie . . .

To be saying something, anything at all, he asked "T-tenements?" Hurrying or no, James's feet were growing colder every minute in the too-large shoes.

"Houses for more than one family." Plumed Hat gave him an odd look. "Are there not such things in Africa?"

"Yes," James said hastily. "I—I just didn't know the word."

This Smithfield turned out to be just that, a field. It was a very large one, though, with stout pens to hold cattle and horses, sheep and pigs, on market days. To their left, the church's gatehouse and St. Bartholomew's hospital faced onto the field, and along the far west side were crowded shops and the tenements above them. James and his rescuer passed along the long right-hand side of the field. When they came to the stone posts of the City barrier—"the bars" that could be linked by chain to close the road—they passed through them and down a street Plumed Hat called "Cowcross" to Turnmill Street.

Cowcross Street . . . Turnmill Street . . . James blinked

and bit back an exclamation. He remembered Cowcross Street from its sign somewhere near the Farringdon Underground station at the foot of Turnmill Street. If the names were the same, perhaps . . .

His mind couldn't reach beyond the *If*.

"Here you are." Plumed Hat pointed up to the right. "Turnmill Street. Follow it to the top and you will see the Clerk's Well beyond the crossroad." He smiled. "Will you go on alone, or shall I come to see you do not topple over in the street?"

"No, I know where I am now," James said quickly. "I can go by myself. Thank—thank you for the clothes and—and everything." He hesitated. "I don't know when I can return them, but . . ."

Plumed Hat was already turning away. "Tomorrow or next week, 'tis no great matter. The Wardrobe Master won't miss 'em." With a wave he turned on his heel and strode at a swift, long-legged pace back the way they had come.

James gave himself a doglike shake and set off up Turnmill Street at a run. At the top he stopped, breathless, and almost laughed aloud. It was there!

The crossroads. The green. The well, and the door in the wall. The road climbing gently toward the tree-crowned rise. He took a deep breath and made for the well, but slowed as he drew near. The door—his door—was closed. A cloaked woman and girl were leaning over the wall to scoop up water with their pitchers and pour it into the tall wooden bucket that stood between them. He wondered if he dared climb onto the well wall while they were there to step across and try whether the door was barred. They finished and slid a pole through the bucket's handle as he reached the corner of the wall, then hoisted it between them and moved off with even, gliding steps, and no sloshing. As they left, though, he had no chance to climb up, for a water-carrier came along the Clerkenwell Road, carrying what looked like a four-foot-tall wooden pitcher on a leather strap across his back. It was made, like a barrel, of staves and iron bands. After him a woman came from one of the houses opposite with a stewing kettle to fill.

James jiggled up and down on his cold feet, unhappy at the thought that he might have to wait until darkness sent people home to their dinners. Hard as it was to be near the stone stairs and the way home, he could not wait there. Five minutes of standing still in the wind off the hill was enough to let the cold creep in. He felt the river-cold shiver stir again under his breastbone and turned away in desperation. With his hands clutching the edges of the cloak and tucked under his armpits, he wheeled and turned the corner to jog along the front wall of what Plumed Hat had called "the old nunnery."

Whatever the original gateway had looked like, it was gone, for the uneven opening had no gateposts, and the high gates propped open in the gap had a makeshift look. James sidled past two cartloads of timber waiting to enter, and once inside caught a glimpse along to his left of the top of the stair—his stair. It looked like nothing more than a narrow passage between the outer wall and the building beside it, but James recognized it at once.

Two steps past the gate, he was stopped.

"Nay, out you go, lad. My lord's orders," rumbled the barrel-shaped gateman. "'No curious passersby,

John Potts,' says he. My lord's laborers and servants only, and trespassers to be charged under the law."

Arguing was no use. The gateman moved him on as if he were an earthscraper and James a very small tree.

James was not stopped for long. The wall met the church only a few yards along the road past the gate, and the door to the church's porch opened at a push. Slipping inside, James crossed the stone flag floor as quietly as he could in the stiff-soled shoes. A few old women and an elderly man sat, heads bowed, on the benches behind the two boxed-in pews at the front. No one turned to look as he slipped back the side aisle and eased open one leaf of the west porch door. It gave a direct view across the path of the timber carts to the top of the stair down to the well. James closed the door gently and moved on to the room at the bottom of the bell tower. Finding an old cloak hanging on a peg there, he wrapped himself in it and sat down in a shadowy corner to wait for darkness.

The old people left. Another old man, in a long black gown, puttered around, straightening benches and snuffing out the candles lit to push back the late-afternoon shadows. Outside, at dusk, the laborers left. The gateman barred the gate and vanished in the gloom. James returned the old cloak to its peg, and when the last sound faded, he opened the west door, closed it, and dashed for the stair.

It was there.

The faintest of shimmers, below the middle landing.

Relief made James's legs feel so wobbly that he had to sit down on the cold stone pavement of the landing to keep them from folding under him. When he caught his breath, he looked more closely, and noticed that the shimmer had shifted to the left since he had last seen it. The edge now touched the outer wall, but when he bent close he could make out in the dim light of dusk a patch of concrete basement floor. The tea chest was not where he had left it, but from above he should not need it.

He stood, moved down one stone step, sat on its edge, swung his legs through the shimmer, folded his arms over his head, hunched down, and rolled forward.

seven

THE BASEMENT FLOOR WAS FARTHER BELOW the shimmer than James expected. His toes touched down, but his curled-up weight pitched him forward, and only the protection of his arms kept his head from a nasty knock. But he was through! And safe.

The basement room was pitch dark, and all James could do was guess about direction and edge forward cautiously, his hands outstretched. When his fingertips met the wall he followed it to the left, but instead of the stair he met the stacked-up empty tea chests. Backtracking along the wall, he found the iron pipe railing and a moment later was standing breathless, his heart hammering, in Cousin Charles's ground-floor hallway. Light filtered down from the skylight high above and confused him for a moment. It had been dusk, almost dark in that other London. . . . But there it was winter, of course, and here was summer!

James sat for almost five minutes on the bottom stair step, taking deep breaths, before he could face the four flights of stairs. At the top the gleaming oak door of Cousin Charles's flat looked so beautiful that James almost kissed it. He rang the bell just in case, but there was no answer, so he reached down to feel in the pocket of his shorts for his key, and only then remembered that he was dressed for a very different London. He wasn't even sure he was still *wearing* his shorts. After a fumble at the thick breeches where the pocket of the shorts underneath would be, his heart sank. No key. It was probably at the bottom of the River Thames.

James was about to sit down in the corner of the little landing to wait when his eye fell on the ficus tree that grew in a large pot beside the door, under the skylight. Cousin Charles had sent Phil Parrett a key to the outer door two weeks ago but was late getting copies made for the key to the flat, so he'd told Phil that the emergency key was hung high in the ficus branches. James's dad had spotted and retrieved it easily enough, but James, being shorter, had to climb up onto the rim of the heavy pot. He held his breath as he searched through the leaves until he spied the brass key on its ring hung on the stub of a twig. It was a wonder his dad had remembered to replace it after he found the three keys Cousin Charles had left for them on the desk in the sitting room. James unlocked the door and then returned the key to its twig.

The flat was quiet. And empty. James looked into the sitting room and each of the bedrooms, the kitchen last. He was relieved, but only for a moment. He had his hand on the refrigerator door's handle—he hadn't eaten since breakfast—when the kitchen wall clock caught his eye. Eleven-thirty. *Eleven-thirty?* That was more than two hours *before* he and Phil stepped onto the footbridge.

The clock must have stopped.

But it hadn't. The second hand was moving.

If the clock was right, then his passage through that other London had somehow taken either less than no time at all, or almost twenty-four hours. Either he hadn't fallen in the river yet, or it had happened yesterday, and his father would be frantic. The police would be trying to find witnesses who'd been on the Millennium Bridge—but even if anyone had been looking in the right place, who was going to pipe up and say, "Yes, I saw it happen. The kid was there—and then he wasn't. Like he fell right through the bridge."

James moved quickly. He opened the fridge to snatch out a bottle of orange juice and the plastic storage box that held cheeses, closed the door, and opened the freezer in search of bread. After staring in for a blank moment, he took out a loaf, closed the door gently, and stood reading the handwritten note on the refrigerator.

Dear Phil and Reenie,

I've stocked the fridge with a few things to hold you until you have a chance to do some shopping. The nearest supermarket is Safeway (on Whitecross Street—see the neighborhood map, and notes on my desk in

the sitting room about shops, decent places
to eat, etc.).

> *Enjoy the flat,*
> *Charles*

It was the note that had been on the refrigerator
door when the Parretts arrived over a week ago. The
note that Phil had crumpled and tossed in the waste-
basket after they had read it.

The food and juice and "long-life" milk were the
food and juice and milk that had been waiting for
them on Monday.

James turned on the TV and sat on the floor by the
coffee table while he enjoyed, bite by slow bite, the
first of the two cheese sandwiches he had made with
bread thawed in the microwave. He watched the tail
end of something called *What If?* while he waited for
the *News at Noon* on Channel 4. If he was right and
the now-today wasn't the same as his this-morning-
today, it could easily be any day between the day
Cousin Charles left for Italy and a week ago Monday,

when James and Reenie and Phil arrived in London. The call asking Reenie whether she could fill in for the injured Nela Androvic on Concentus's six-week tour had come on May 27, almost two and a half weeks ago. And when called the next day about the flat, Cousin Charles had said he was leaving London in two days. . . .

". . . News at Noon," the television intoned, "for Monday, the second of June."

June second. They had arrived on the second.

They had arrived today.

They had arrived today. . . .

James hugged his knees and rocked back and forth in agitation. Today! What was he supposed to do? *What?*

It was three minutes past twelve. Any minute now he was going to walk in on himself, and what would happen then? Would one or the other of him blink out of existence, or would a goggle-eyed Reenie and Phil be stuck forever with both of him? He needed time to think. He certainly didn't want to be the one who blinked out, and just as much didn't like the idea of sharing his parents, his room at home, or any of his grandparents with an eerie double of himself. His old friend Tyrone was always saying that this or that "really creeps me out." Well, Tyrone didn't *know* what it felt like to be creeped out!

He would have to go back down to the basement, sit down, and calmly figure out what to do.

He looked around wildly. Bread crumbs . . . He brushed up all he saw on the counter. Juice bottle . . . Knife into the dishwasher. Bread back into the freezer . . . Juice, cheese, mustard . . . He wrapped his second cheese sandwich in a paper napkin and stuck it inside his jacket.

He wished he still had his watch. As the thought flicked through his mind, he automatically rubbed his wrist and then patted his pockets—or where pockets should have been. But the watch must have been at the bottom of the long-ago river. Without it, the next time he came back he would have to come all the way up, get the key, and come into the flat again to find out what day and time it was. Maybe there was a digital clock, one that registered the date, that he could take to the basement and leave there. Perhaps the stainless one on the sitting room bookshelf. It looked as if it folded flat.

James was in the bathroom, trying not to look at the strangely dressed self in the full-length mirror who was struggling to retie the last laces on his padded breeches, when through the high, partly open window he heard the by-now familiar diesel purr of a taxi. It sounded as if it were drawing up in front of the building, and he raced back to the sitting room and across to the front windows to see. Peering down, he could see his father's lanky form unfolding itself out of the back seat. Fascination almost rooted him there, but horror pushed him back, and in a panicky jumble of the two, he snatched the thin steel clock from the bookcase and ran to the closet by the front door to pull down from the shelf a warm fleece lap rug. Clicking the lock button on the front door, he darted out, slammed it shut behind him, and plummeted down the stairs four steps at a time. Below the second landing he nearly missed his footing and had to slow a little, so that he barely made it to the bottom and the back hallway before he heard the *snick!* of the key in the lock.

• • •

James sat sideways on the top step of the basement stair, with his ear to the door, craning to hear the muffled voices, footsteps on the stairs, and wheeled suitcases bumping upward. The door to the flat was too far above. He could not hear it close.

He sat in the dark for a while, and shifted only to pull the folded blanket under him for a seat. With his elbows on his knees and his chin in his hands, he studied the faint circle he had tumbled through less than an hour before. He had no idea what he was going to do. *Something*, but what? If the shimmer could land him here and now, almost two weeks before he fell into the other London, how could he ever trust it? He stood and pulled the light cord.

The tea chest stood off to one side of the circle, where James supposed a caretaker must have placed it. Otherwise, with no James to move it, it would have been in the corner with the others. James frowned as he sat down again and tried to remember everything he could about the first time he had dreamed The Dream. The sound of water had awakened him; he had come down, seen the circle, crossed into the well's world, and returned before the sun came up. After half an hour? About that. The circle had been smack in the center of the doorway both coming and going. *And* there had been an almost-full moon there. Three nights later he "dreamed" it again. The same time, about two-thirty; down the stairs, through the shimmer—no, move the chest back into place, then go through. Up the moonlit hill took—what, an hour? And there was moonlight, but not a full moon. He came back at dawn. . . .

James sat up straight. At dawn *there*. But it had been dark when he fell back into bed here. *It had been dark, and afterward—five minutes? half an hour?—he had pressed the tiny light button and looked at his watch.* To see how long it would be before he had to get up. And the bright watch face had read 2:05. *2:05.* He must have been so sleepy that he hadn't thought twice about being back in his bed up to half an hour before he had left it. Why should he? It was all a dream, wasn't it?

James chewed at his lower lip. Great. What time he went through, or how long he stayed, must have nothing to do with when he got back. So what did?

The moon? The tea chest? What he had for dinner?

The tea chest . . .

James crossed the room to stare at the circle in the air. Forget the tea chest. Look at the shimmer. The shimmer had moved to the left, so that it touched the wall here, too.

If the shimmer was always shifting, at least it was fixed in the same *place* on the two different worlds—or the two different times. He could go back through and try again. He could even *keep* trying, but if the first try or two didn't work, what was he going to use for food after the second cheese sandwich gave out?

James turned off the light and went around the shimmer—the portal—to look up the stair leading to the old nunnery complex. By starlight he could make out the bare crowns of the trees between the top of the stair passage and the old church. He could go through now, but it was winter there, not June—or it had been. He could smell the cold air, and decided that a basement in June was going to be a lot better than a fleece lap rug in a freezing cold church corner. James shivered at the thought.

Shivered, and then yawned. Spending his day in parts of three different days had left him thoroughly confused about how many hours his awake-in-his-own-skin day had added up to since breakfast. Eight? Ten? Twelve? He looked at the clock he held. 12:38. But that was 12:38 on their arrival-in-London day, not the footbridge day.

Middle of the day or not, he was suddenly, overwhelmingly, sleepy. He folded the fleece square in half and spread it and the woolen cloak on the floor on a spot from which he could watch the stairs and sky. Once down, he tried to find a comfortable position, but could not, so he settled uneasily on his side to face the shimmer, with the clock lying flat on the floor close by. *I should've brought a pillow*, he thought, and in the next moment was asleep.

When he woke, a pale wash of gray had crept up the sky behind the bare treetops. He scrambled to his knees and looked at the clock. To his surprise he had been asleep for seven hours, and the shimmer had moved again. He could see that it now hung three or four inches away from the stone wall it had been touching. That must mean something, but he had no time to puzzle over it. He had to reach the church before the workers showed up, but first he needed a hiding place for the clock. He needed it to tell him what day and time it was when he returned, because if Reenie and Phil—and he—were in the flat, he would have no other safe way to find out.

In summer the building's caretaker probably came only on garbage collection day. He wouldn't go near the central heating system. James turned the light back on and settled for a gap in the mortar between the concrete blocks high up behind the boiler, in the shadow cast by the water pipes. He tore a wide strip off a cleaning rag draped over the sink and wrapped the clock in it, then tucked the thin parcel in out of sight. He left a bit of the cloth sticking out to make it easier to pull free, then folded the fleece throw, tucked it under his arm, turned out the light, dragged the tea chest once again to the opening onto the stair landing in that other place, and climbed through.

eight

ONCE INSIDE THE CHURCH, JAMES TURNED THE KEY in the lock and made his way back to his corner, which was more a niche between the two clusters of stone columns. Pulling the cloak close around him, he sat on one end of the fleece square and wrapped the rest over his knees and under his feet. The air and the stone-flagged floor seemed less cold than before, and after he finished off the sadly mashed cheese sandwich, he settled down to wait for the sounds of work outside and some sign of life in the church. He could easily enough unlock the door into the street, since the old man in the black nightgown outfit had left the key in the lock, but that might make Black Nightgown more careful with his keys. Besides, the thought of stepping out into the street at all was unsettling. Here, as in the Clerkenwell base-ment, he felt cut adrift from both worlds. Safer. Almost as if time held its breath, as if it could not touch him.

Well, he was, wasn't he? Adrift in time. Or in some alternate world, like in some of the old *Star Trek* episodes.

Adrift, anyway.

He dozed off and never heard the creak of the gates as they opened, or the rumble of cart wheels. The sounds of saws and hammering wove themselves into his dreaming. It was only the padding footsteps of Black Nightgown and the scraping of the oversize key in first one lock and then the other that startled him awake. Once Black Nightgown vanished through a small side door up at the altar end of the church, James stood and stretched. He folded the gray lap rug twice lengthwise, rolled it up tightly, and crammed it up behind the wing stumps of a battered stone angel that stood between two of the half-columns spaced around the walls of the bell tower room. He stood listening for a moment, and when he heard only silence, crossed to the main door and slipped out. As he went, his eye slid across and then back to an elegantly handwritten notice pinned to a board on the doorpost:

Parish Church of St. John
First Sabbath after Advent
Services, Nine of the Clock,
Eleven, and Three

James stared at it numbly. *Advent.* That meant Christmas season. The first time had felt like bitter February. Not that it mattered, he thought bleakly. What mattered—*all* that mattered—was getting through the day and back to the well stairs before nightfall.

The sky in the east was washed with a pale gold, clear and hard as glass, that dimmed to gray toward the west. James felt a little lightheaded. The colorless sunshine, the horsemen, creaking carts, passersby cloaked and shawled against the cold, were solid but seemed unreal. This crossroads, this wide place where Clerkenwell Road divided to run along both sides of a trampled island of grass, was Clerkenwell Green. Looking down to the west where the road crossed a bridge over a narrow stream, he was looking toward the bridge that crossed over the Underground train tracks, then climbed toward Theobald's Road and Oxford Street, the Virgin Superstore, and the military miniatures shop in St. Christopher's Place. Eerie!

The safest thing to do, he decided, was to retrace his steps of his winter-yesterday, so as not to get lost. He wondered vaguely whether he was now in the December after the January or February when he dropped into the river, or the one before—or some other year altogether. Not that it mattered.

He angled across the road to follow Turnmill Street downward past its prosperous-looking houses, and here and there a high garden wall. He did not pay much attention to them or the women hanging out of upstairs windows to call to passersby, and noticed only distantly that the muddy street was already noisy and busy. The mud of the street had an unpleasant smell that made him cover his nose and mouth, but no one else seemed to notice it. Near Cowcross Street a rising sound of honking and muttering made James turn around to see a large flock of geese gaining on him. He retreated to a doorstep to watch a man and woman and three children herd them past. The geese, two hundred at least, marched along to their fates with a businesslike waggle of white tails and waddle of blackened feet. Market. They had to be going to market at Smithfield. That explained the crowd. James quickened his pace when he stepped back into the street.

At Smithfield more farmers, animals, and buyers poured in, pushing past him, though the great field was already crowded with buyers, bawling cattle, pens crowded with bleating sheep and squealing pigs. Chickens were crammed into basketwork cages, and ducks and geese penned inside circles of willow fencing. The hubbub of sounds and smells beat at James's senses, and he found himself stepping more briskly and looking more sharply. Outside the inns and taverns facing the great market, men drank and talked business, argued and bargained. From inside one tavern, men's voices bawled out the notes of a song and were answered as loudly by another group in what sounded like a sort of singing war. All James could catch of the words was something about "angels' food" and "angels' wine." Women hurried by, carrying under their arms, or by cords around the legs, squawking chickens or protesting ducks. Two furious young men faced off in a shouting match. A milky-eyed old woman guided by a small black girl felt the udders and bony back of a milk goat and haggled over a price. In the moment when James recognized that she was black, he was already past and she was out of sight. It happened so quickly that he wondered whether he had imagined her. Here and there, always in the thickest press of people, he saw ragged figures moving through like eels who reminded him of some in the hard-faced ragged host he had seen sweeping down the long moonlit slope into the city on his second night's visit. Was that what they were? A tribe of thieves? For a moment he thought he had seen one slice a man's purse from his belt as he slid past, but if he had, it was done too neatly to be sure.

James was fascinated by everything, and at the same time uneasy. He wasn't sure why. He tried to think, but in that hubbub it was a while before he realized what he was seeing. At home, at least anywhere *he* went, he had never been in a next-to-all-white world, or even an all-white crowd, though a few Boston concert audiences came close. Here he didn't see a face that *wasn't* white—though some, peering out of raggedy bundles of clothes, were so grimy he had to take a second look. Then he began to notice eyes. Instead of the unseeing, inward, my-mind-is-somewhere-else gazes of the hurrying city crowds he knew, these eyes were roving, watchful or wary, curious, fierce or humorous, or shuttered, but still alive to every face and movement. No one seemed to be running on autopilot except for some with the numb look of illness or bone-weariness, and the bleary drunks with a head start on the day's drinking.

He wasn't invisible. That was it. He had always felt safely invisible, unseen or ignored, in crowds. Now he saw startled looks, but no hostile stares that turned away or nervous ones that flinched aside. A few glances did slide by him, detached and supercilious, but what he saw was curiosity. Curiosity on all sides. And one sour-faced man who muttered, "Foreigners!" and spat as he shouldered past.

It was a relief to reach Long Lane, which was busy, but not so crowded. James had not gone far when he was stopped, startled by the sound from farther up the lane of a boy's voice declaiming loudly something he could not make out. As he moved on, another answered with, "A mellifluous voice, as I am a true knight!"

"A contagious breath," boomed the first, in a fair imitation of a man's voice. It was answered by the second with, "Very sweet and contagious, i' faith."

The first voice, picking up the pace, rattled off, "To hear by the nose, it is dulcet in contagion. But shall we make the welkin dance indeed? Shall we rouse the night-owl in a catch that will—" The speaker took a breath. "—draw three souls out of one weaver? Shall we do that?"

"Well spoke!" a man called out.

The speeches—from a play, James guessed—flew faster, and he craned to see ahead, but a cartload of small birds in cages blocked his view.

"An you love me, let's do't: I am a dog at a catch."

"By'r lady, sir, and some dogs will catch well," mocked the first voice James had heard.

"Most certain. Let our catch be, 'Thou knave,'" crowed the second.

As the cart pulled ahead, the speakers came into

view, striding—and occasionally hopping—toward Smithfield. James saw two boys, a skinny one of about twelve in a scarlet cloak trimmed in gold braid, and a shorter, chunkier one who might even so have been a year older, in a blue cloak with a black and silver badge. The boy in scarlet gave a scornful laugh. "'Twas a play not worth my penny. How can you like it? Why, it is full of fools and knaves, with no cure for 'em!"

The chunky boy in blue grew red-faced. "It made me laugh," he said. "I liked it!"

"You tell 'im, me dear," called a stout, red-cheeked dame in a quilted, fur-trimmed velvet cloak.

The thin boy put on a wounded look and kissed his hand and pressed it to his heart with such a wild, woeful lover's rolling eye and heaving sigh that both the stout lady and the boy in blue melted into giggles.

"Give us the clown's song!" someone cried. "Give us 'When that I was a little tiny boy!'"

When that I was a little tiny boy? James's heart gave a leap.

Before either of the two boys could answer, James startled himself, the boys, and the passersby by singing out, in the high, clear treble he had come to hate,

When that I was and a tiny little boy,
With hey, ho, the wind and the rain,
A foolish thing was but a toy,
For the rain it raineth every day . . .

The song was one Reenie had sung to him at bedtime when he was small, and the impulse that made it leap out in the middle of a crowd was so unexpected that he stopped abruptly after the first verse, as alarmed as he was confused and embarrassed. With a hasty nod, he sidestepped past the boys and hurried on. He strode quickly, head down, eyes on the paving stones. He certainly didn't need to attract any more attention than his dark skin drew just by being there. He tried walking with his eyes on the ground, but that way he could not see people approaching until their skirts or feet appeared and he had to swerve aside, so he gave up and looked up.

In front of him, dancing along backward, was young Blue Cloak, his face eager with curiosity.

"You *are* an African! Are you? You are! I've never seen an African close-to before. Where did you learn that tune for the song from Master Shakespeare's new play? 'Tis not the tune I heard."

"My mother sings it that way," James said shortly, refusing to slow down. Blue Cloak kept up his nimble, backward dance.

"Your mother! Do Africans sing English songs, then?"

"No—*yes*, but—look, will you *stop* that?" James demanded in frustration. "I'm—I'm in a hurry."

"To go where?" Blue Cloak stopped his backward dance and came to walk beside James. "I'm late off to school already. I'll go with you."

James slowed a little. Maybe it wasn't a bad idea. At least he wouldn't need to worry about getting lost. "St. Paul's," he said reluctantly.

"Oh!" The boy looked even more cheerful. "Then you go the long way. Come with me. I'll show you the shorter way, and not be so much late to school, and so earn only a small beating. Master Talley's hand is light, and my breeches and hose thick. Come!"

"Your teachers beat you?" James asked, startled. Gran Parrett had told him that she once was paddled in school for not doing her homework, and he had thought she was making it up. He wondered now whether her teacher's hand had been "light."

"Of course." The boy cocked his head. "Do not the teachers in Africa beat their pupils?"

"Not where I come from," James said, sidestepping a lie.

The boy's eyes grew wide. "Oh, I should like that above all things! I am not wicked, but I spatter ink sometimes, and spoil my paper, or my hose droop, or I make mistakes in my Latin sentences. My father calls me a flibbertigibbet!"

James decided his father might be right, but did not say so.

As they went, the boy was full of questions. "What is your name? I am Thomas. Thomas Clifton."

"James Parrett."

"Parrett? And James? But, 'tis an English name! Your father—he is one of the venturers to lands like Africa or America, then?"

"He teaches music," James answered reluctantly,

not sure he should tell even that much. *Don't say a word you don't have to. You'll put your foot in it.*

"A teacher of music? But how, then, did he meet your mother? Did she come with one of the embassies to London? Is she a princess? Is she as black as the night, and beautiful?"

James blinked and said nothing. But even silence, he found, was enough to start a new avalanche of questions, about the fabulous treasures to be found in Africa or America, or the uncanny or terrible creatures, or the vast unexplored forests.

By the time the two boys came to the end of the lane and turned, James had learned—without asking—that Thomas's father was a gentleman of importance (Thomas's words) in Norfolk; that he had a fine house and farms; that he rented the house in Long Lane and brought Thomas and his mother south away from the bitter northeastern winter; that Christchurch school, where Thomas was a pupil, was the best of—

"Where has your friend gone?" James asked hastily as Thomas drew a deep breath and was about to plunge on.

"My friend? Oh, the redbird." Thomas shrugged. "He stopped me this morning and wanted to talk about plays I liked. I've seen him before, but I don't know who he is, except that he is one of the Children. They think themselves little lords, our schoolmasters say."

James turned a blank look on him. "'One of the Children'? What do you mean? *You're* a child."

Thomas laughed. "Not 'children.' *Children*. Children of the Chapel Royal. Crimson is the queen's servants' color. They sing in the queen's chapel choir and they act in plays. They—"

James interrupted again as they reached the end of the lane, and Smithfield. "Where to now?"

"This way, past St. Bartholomew's gatehouse, and down Little Britain." Thomas pointed left around the corner. "Through the alleys behind the hospital is a yard, and a little gate through the City wall that leads into the old monastery. In the old days it was a private passage for the monks, but my school at Christchurch is there now, and we use it. I can show you the way through and out to the street near to St. Paul's."

As they passed into another narrow street, from some-where nearby a bell began to toll the hour. Thomas gave a startled hop and snatched at James's cloak. "Come, run! Here's our alley! Come—if I am through the door before the last knell, I won't be beat! An' if you slip through the church and on out," he panted as he ran, "you'll see St. Paul's tower. . . . Once you're in the street . . . it's only across the Shambles . . . and down Ivy Lane."

James followed him into a passage crowded on both sides by buildings. Ahead, other boys were running. Thomas and James appeared to be last, but at the second corner James turned his head and saw one coming up behind.

It was just then that it happened. Two men stepped out from a shadowy doorway and caught hold of Thomas by one arm and by his cloak. Thomas was running so fast that he was swung around and slammed into the passage wall. Two more men appeared from a side passage.

"Hey!" James shouted, and leaped to grab at the nearest man's arm. "Let him go!"

The man flung him off. "Away with you, blackie," he grated. "Get away! This is no affair of yours."

"No!" The shout came from behind.

The skinny boy Thomas had named "one of the Children" came running up. He had turned his cloak buff-colored side out, but the scarlet and gold flashed as he ran.

"No! Take him, too. Take the African!"

nine

"LET—ME—GO!" JAMES SHOUTED. HE STRUGGLED, but the man who held him from behind had his upper arms in a grip that left him helpless. He tried to stamp on the man's foot, but missed. "We don't have any money! Let us go!"

The taller, dark-bearded man of the second two laughed. "Master Blackamoor takes you for a footpad, Gowthrop. Stop his mouth. But only for the moment, mind."

The man holding James released his right arm and clapped a cold hand over his mouth. James tried to tug it away, but his arm was so sore and his hand so numbed that he could not pry loose even a finger. He kicked backward and connected with the man's knee, but he was off-balance and the kick had no force. The man simply ignored him. Thomas, who was holding his bloody nose and breathing through his mouth, swiveled his head to stare dumbly from one man to another.

The men looked too neat and respectably dressed, and the second two too prosperous, to be thieves. The one who had spoken wore a wide, flat sort of velvet cap, an earring, and a white, pleated ruff around his neck, and he held a plum-colored cloak wrapped tightly around him. His stouter, older companion was dressed in a long green gown under his brown cloak. His velvet cap was brown and his ruff smaller, but the sleeves under his cloak were trimmed with silver lace. He stood, arms crossed, and beamed at the boys as if, James thought, he and Thomas were trophies in some game. The other two men seemed to be servants.

The dark-bearded man pulled from under his cloak and unfolded a piece of paper or parchment and read it off with the self-important air of a man making a proclamation, "Know this: that on behalf of Nathaniel Giles, Master of the Children of the Chapel Royal, I claim you, Thomas Clifton, and you—"

James, with a large hand over his mouth, could

only glare, so Dark Beard looked questioningly at Thomas instead. Thomas, with a hopeless look, let go his nose long enough to take a bloody snuffle and mumble miserably, "James. James Parrett."

"Thank you, Master Clifton. And you, James Parrett, to serve as choristers in Her Majesty's Chapel Royal, being—" He read again from the parchment, "so authorized, and having this our present commission with him to take such and so many children as he, or his sufficient deputy shall think meet . . . within this our realm of England, whatsoever they be. And so forth, and so forth." He folded up the commission and tucked it away inside the coat of his suit. "Gentlemen, shall we go?"

Thomas walked meekly between Dark Beard, whose name was Robinson, and Brown Cloak, whom he addressed as Will Topliffe. Gowthrop and Buswell, the two serving men, followed with James held firmly between them. Buswell, the younger and cheerier of the two, shook his head pityingly each time James felt one of them relax and tried to struggle free.

"Ch! Do be kind to yourself, young master. 'Tis no

use to kick against the pricks, as horsemen say. You do go to a good life, with food aplenty—and not all soused pork! Ask Jack Garland yonder. Last week there was venison, and turkey is promised the Children for Christmas. There's fine clothes to strut in and robes to sing in, and masters to school you—if Master Giles decides to keep you."

"He will when he has heard this parrot sing," put in the scarlet-coated boy, who was following close behind. He grinned at his own pun.

"You heard but one verse from one song," Thomas protested bravely. "What's that?"

"Hold your tongue, Cockroach," the boy the men called Garland whispered back fiercely. "I have heard the African sing more, but I was where I should not have been, so Master Giles cannot know the where and when."

James heard, but was too frantic at the thought of being hauled off to wherever the queen lived in this here-and-now to worry about a new puzzle. Her palace could be miles away, in Westminster, like the palace in the other—in his—London. Finding his way back to Clerkenwell Close would be a nightmare. He set himself to watching every turn they made and trying to remember every street name on a house corner, but too many street corners had none. Here and there, though, where houses were not built up against each other, he caught glimpses of the old City wall where it ran along the backs of yards and gardens.

He forced himself to think more calmly. The sun was on their left, so they were walking south, toward the river, not west. If they were to be taken away west, wouldn't they have been bundled into a coach before this? He began to think that it might not be a bad thing to be off the strange streets and out of the cold at least until afternoon. And lunch. If they gave him lunch, there might be something he could slip into his pocket for a supper once he was back in the church in Clerkenwell and waiting for the workers to leave. Little by little, he relaxed.

The straggly little procession passed the remnant of the old City gateway at Newgate Street and at the next cross street turned in through a second great gateway at Ludgate. From there they threaded their way

through narrow streets to an even narrower passageway off Carter Lane. James was near panic again. So
many corners turned! How could he remember?

The passageway opened into a large courtyard bordered by large old buildings built of stone, one with
tall windows with pointed arches, like a church's. From
there came the sound, muffled by thick stone walls, of
singing. The stone walls may have stopped the words,
but the strong, clear notes swelled and rang against the
windowpanes and out into the wintry air: boys' voices,
and some men's, and the sound of stringed instruments,
and a trumpet so golden sweet in tone that it made
James's unwilling heart stir in wonder.

James and Thomas were led across and up broad
steps between the tall columns of a newly plastered
and painted building, and in at an arched doorway.
There they were hurried along a hallway hung with
colorful silk banners to a huge, dim room furnished
only with a few chairs and a table by the one window.
They were ordered to wait. While they fidgeted
nervously, they could hear voices ringing out in the
room beyond—first something that sounded to a

puzzled James like "all your potatoes or oyster pies in the world," and then a furious "No, no! The child speaks as shyly as a maid. And *lisps*. It will not do!"

A murmur followed, and a new voice snapped, "Excellent. Bring them in."

Mr. Robinson reappeared, and motioned Thomas and James through the open door. He gave both an impatient push as Thomas, in front, hung back.

"Master Giles, here are Thomas Clifton and James Parrett."

James darted a quick look around the room, as large as the first, with richly paneled walls and carved ceiling beams. It was lit by windows on each side and fires in two great fireplaces. Like the first room, its floor was covered with a carpeting of loose rushes— a sort of "fat grass" was what it looked like to James. At the far end a door led into a third room. James could hear, dimly, the sound of voices—one, then others, apparently answering in unison. In the room he had just entered, four men stood talking in a far corner. Three others, in crimson coats much like the boy Garland's, sat on stools nearby, and two on the benches at a table more than twenty feet long that stood near the brightest window. Two boys, one in a blue coat identical to Thomas's, with the same black and silver badge, stood in the center of the room. Each held a thin sheaf of papers, and both gave the newcomers a startled, hopeful look that faded to disappointment when they saw the four men who pushed in behind James and Thomas.

The tall, bearded man who stood at the head of the room, not far from the door, turned to sweep the two boys with a dark-browed frown. He wore a gown of plum-colored velvet with gold lace at the wrists, and a neat ruff of sparkling whiteness at his neck.

"Ah, good. The Christchurch lad. The one I saw in the Plautus last spring term?"

"Y-yes, sir. But I wasn't much good."

"I shall decide that."

"B-but, sir?" Thomas wavered. "I cannot stay. My father is a gentleman, and he will not like it."

It was as if he had not spoken. The Master turned away to say, "What think you, Poet?"

A tall, brown-suited, ungainly man with a thick

body and long, thin arms and legs sat scribbling at a table. Looking up, he grimaced. "I think if he reads poorly, he will yet serve well enough as the Perfumer. If badly, he can be one of the mutes. Miracle, perhaps. Or Time. But—ho!"

He heaved himself up and crossed to stoop and stare eye to eye with James, then pulled him forward. "What lad is this, shrinking back behind Robinson, Master? It seems your son-in-law has trolled his line in the water and hooked a young African!"

"So he has!" Giles turned to the four child-takers. "Where did you scoop him up? And why?"

Jack Garland, the red-coated boy from Long Lane, stepped forward. "He can sing, Master Giles. Young Clifton there may make a pretty girl upon a stage, but the blackamoor can sing."

James's eyes flicked from one face to another. Sing? He didn't sing. Wouldn't sing. *Didn't, wouldn't, couldn't! He had to be in Clerkenwell before dark.* He was startled to realize that in the last hour he had forgotten that already. But just as quickly he forgot what he had forgotten, for he saw a familiar face at the far side of the room.

Plumed Hat.

Plumed Hat stood talking with three other men, gesturing, shaking his head, his velvet hat with the green ostrich plume tucked under his arm. Then with a nod he turned and crossed toward the door. As he slipped behind the Master and out, his eyes fell on James, but there was no recognition in them, only a flicker of curiosity.

So I must not have fallen in the river yet. . . .

James dragged his attention back to Master Giles, who was stroking his pointed salt-and-pepper beard and eyeing him doubtfully. "So he may, Garland, but 'tis players I need first. As to that, I don't deny he's a likely looking lad, and would show well in white and gold, or that we have been short four of the twenty-four characters our poet has on stage in Act Five, but—"

"But he is a *blackamoor!*" protested a stout, perspiring gentleman who sat at a small table near the Master, and too near the fire. The goose-quill pen in his hand hovered over the column of figures he had been adding.

"I had noticed, friend Evans," Nathaniel Giles

said dryly. "But we play our *Cynthia's Revels* before the queen on Twelfth Night, not four weeks off. There is the choir to prepare for daily and Sundays' chapel services, and but five days before the public comes to view friend Jonson's play. If the boy can act and sing, I would not care if he were a Chinaman." He looked thoughtful. "The queen, indeed, might well be pleased. The great John Blanke, trumpeter to her father and grandfather, was African and she has African dancers and a passable singer or two in her service. But—no. My warrant to take children is for Her Majesty's subjects only, not foreigners. We'll be content with young Clifton and these other three. You, son-in-law, give him a sixpence for his trouble and send him on his way."

Mr. Robinson nodded. "I will, but Master—the boy says his name is James Parrett."

The poet wrinkled up his nose. "Parrot? Spelled how? I know of a Parrot. 'Tis a name that can stink up a more larger room than this."

"It's P-A-R-R-E-T-T," James said warily, hoping that wasn't the smelly spelling.

"Excellent!" The poet smiled down at James from his gangly height. "Then I say, Welcome, James Parrett."

The stout gentleman, a Mr. Evans, frowned. "Parrett. 'Tis no African name."

"Poh!" the poet exclaimed. "A splash of milk in his wine punch! Did I not say so?" he boomed out with a wave of an arm. He had not said so, but no one corrected him, though one or two of the men in back rolled their eyes.

"Have you no eyes in your heads? The child does not carry himself like an African." The big man straightened to his full height to cross the room and back, and as he did so, his ungainly arms and burly shoulders shook off their round-shouldered stoop and took on a proud and lionhearted stately ease. The transformation was startling and impressive, and then was gone. The poet came to stand in front of James with his hands on his hips, to stare down at him.

James stared back, taking in the pockmarked face, the untidy hair, and the brown suit that bore the grease stains of a careless breakfast. He also saw that the oddly uneven eyes were looking *at* him, not just in his direction, like most people's. One eye was a little lower, one a little larger, but they were guessing, adding up, wondering—*interested*.

"Parrett, eh? Your father is English, then. Where were you born? Here or in Africa?"

"In America," James said without thinking.

It was an answer that fizzed around the room like an electric current. Eyes widened, feet shifted, bodies leaned forward, and James—a little late—had a moment of panic as he wondered what year it was, and whether the English had been to America yet or just heard rumors of it. He had leapfrogged the question about his dad's being English (*well, Grandpa Parrett was born English and didn't see America until he was five. . . .*), and landed right in it. But no—it was all right. "Africa or America," young Thomas had said. Still, being careful was going to be hard. Everything was so new and strange that curiosity tingled through his veins like an electric buzz he couldn't shut off.

"In America!" The poet gave a shout of laughter. "An African Englishman from the Savage Paradise! I like this one, liar or no. Let's have him, Master Giles. If he reads well, he can play a part in my satire. If not, you can give him a song or two." Returning to the table, he drew a sheet from a pile weighted down with a candlestick. "Here, young Parrett. Parrot me this. From here," he tapped the page, "to the bottom, where it reads 'Exit.'"

James frowned at the paper. The handwriting was neat, but full of curlicue letters and hard to decipher, and the sentences seemed uncomfortably curlicued, too. After a long moment James began, slowly.

> *If gracious silence, sweet attention,*
> *Quick sight, and quicker apprehension,*
> *The light of judgment's . . .*

"No, no, *no!*" The poet whirled away and flung himself down again in his chair. "Hopeless accent, deadly earnestness. We must make an end of it, and have Pykman and Grimes, and perhaps Trussell, double up on parts. A great pity. It would have been a pretty stroke to have my Cupid be an African."

Master Giles waved an impatient hand. "Can you use him or not, Benjamin?"

"Yes, yes. At worst he can be Thauma, who does not speak."

"His father is a teacher of music!" Thomas piped up, to James's alarm. Thomas clearly never knew when or how to hold his tongue.

"Excellent!" exclaimed the Master. "The boy is schooled, and reads music, then."

James said nothing, but scowled at being talked about over his own head as if he were invisible. Already he disliked the Master.

"That's settled, then," the poet said. He went to his table and took up one of the sheaves of paper pinned together at the corner, then turned back to the Master.

Thomas pulled back, but was pushed forward willy-nilly. When the Master put out his hand and said, "Here, Benjamin, give me the lines," Thomas refused to take the pages held out to him.

"I cannot," he croaked, and swallowed hard. "My father will not like it. My father is a gentleman, and he—"

"I do not care whether your father be lord or laborer. Her Majesty's warrant has given you to me."

Giles drew Thomas forward and thrust the papers into his hand, but just then loud voices sounded in the outer hallway and burst through into the next room. With a shout of, "He will see me whether he wishes or no!" a stout man in a furred gown and cloak and a padded black velvet cap with flaps over his ears burst into the room. His face was flushed with anger.

"Where is this Giles?" He pushed past Mr. Robinson and the others like a bull through a willow fence. "And where is my son? Ah, Thomas. Good!" He came to a stop before the Master of the Children, the only one who did not step back in the face of his charge. The Master held Thomas fast by his arm.

"You are Giles, the master here?"

"I am."

"Sir, my name is Henry Clifton. The Master of Christchurch has sent in haste to tell me that your confederates snatched my son, this boy, from the street this morning on his way to school. Two of his schoolfellows heard and saw it." With an effort, he mastered his anger. "I am come to take him home, sir. You will please release him."

Giles's voice was cold. "My apologies, Master Clifton, but I will not. I had warrant from Her Majesty to take him, and my warrant says that I may keep him."

Thomas's father was not a tall man, but he drew himself up with a dignity that was more impressive than the Master's arrogance. "I am not without friends, sir," he said. "If I must, I shall make complaint to some I know on the Queen's Council, and they will call you to account. *Sir*."

The Master flushed. He made a sign to Mr. Robinson, who moved to his side and pulled Thomas a few steps back toward the windows. "Complain to whom you wish, Mr. Clifton," he snapped. "We will defend our action and, by heaven, if the queen is persuaded not to uphold her warrant to us, she must find another Master for her service."

Mr. Clifton, if he was startled by such strong words, bravely answered them. "You have your pride, sir, but so do I. It cannot be fitting for a gentleman of my estate to have his son and heir forced to so low a calling as 'player.'"

The Master glowered. "You think too well of yourself, sir. We have authority enough to press any nobleman's son in England into our service." He turned and thrust the scroll again at Thomas.

"Let us hear you now, Clifton. The part marked *Echo*. From the top of the scroll."

Thomas, frightened, looked to his father.

"Do not look to your father," the Master ordered. "Read, or be whipped."

Henry Clifton stared at the Master's back, then, white with anger, turned to go. "I will be back, Thomas," he said loudly, and slammed the heavy oak door behind him.

James wavered between fascination and fear as he watched the miserable Thomas, sniffling as he read the lines. The fascination was with this vivid, dangerous world he had stumbled—well, stepped—into. The fear was that with no father to rescue him he might never get the chance to step back out of it.

ten

WHEN JAMES LOOKED AGAIN IT WAS THE POET, Benjamin Jonson, who had taken Thomas in charge. He had pulled a stool close to the window and sat with a frown of concentration and now and again a nod as he listened to Thomas read. Thomas had stopped sniffling, but more than once cast a longing look toward the door.

James did, too, but did not realize that he was shifting from one foot to the other until a man in the red and gold coat of the Chapel Royal appeared beside him. He looked amused.

"Come with me." He took James's elbow and steered him out the door and through to the outer room. On the left a door led into the hallway of an outer building. Immediately across that hallway was a busy kitchen. The man led James down the hall to the left and pointed to the last door.

"The privy," he said. "I'll wait."

James smothered a snort of laughter as the door shut behind him. The privy was what Reenie in a jokey mood called a "comfort station," but the only comfort it offered was a long wooden four-hole seat fitted over the chillier old stone version. The narrow slit of a window was open to the outside for ventilation, so the air was frigid. While he fumbled at retying the laces on his breeches with cold fingers, James slipped along to the slit for a look outside. He could not see much more than that it opened onto a passageway between buildings.

His guide was waiting in the entry hall, arms crossed against the cold. "I am Dick Plumley, by the by," he announced. "Gentleman of the Chapel, singing man. Come. Once the last of the speaking parts for friend Jonson's revel all are parceled out, the Master will have you new lads up to join the others to step out the movements on the stage so you'll have 'em in mind as you learn your speeches. Never worry, if you're to be Thauma. Thauma doesn't say a word."

When they reached the foot of the great stair, the Master was already on his way up, with the boys and several of the men following. Through the door at the top of the stairs, James was astonished to find himself looking down the length of the most amazing theatre he had ever seen. Long and high-ceilinged, it was lit by tall, diamond-paned windows along each side, and was a dazzle of columns, galleries, high, springing beams, and rich carving. Two great gold-leafed chandeliers hung over the stage, and candelabra were fixed all along the three galleries that rose along the other three sides of the hall. With the rows of benches in the center and those in the galleries, there must have been seating for five hundred. The walls—and much else—were painted white; the ceiling was pale blue; and the columns, paneling, beams, and other woodwork blue or crimson, green or yellow, or purple and gold. The open-area stage and stage galleries at the far end were even more elaborate than the boxes and galleries for the audience. The great room was meant to dazzle, and it did.

So did the voices that soared up to the pale blue ceiling. James recognized the melody first, and then the thread of words that wove the voices, bass and tenor, alto, and treble together, repeating and echoing. The wording was different but there was no mistaking the tune to Psalm 100, "Old Hundredth."

> O enter then his gates with praise,
> Approach with joy his courts unto:
> Praise, laud, and bless his name always
> For it is seemly so to do.

James's granddad had taught his own gospel version of the psalm to his Galilee Choir when James was small. He wondered what the Master would think if he heard that rhythm-and-echo version shouted out by twenty five- and six-year-olds.

The children of the Chapel Royal choir were lined up in two rows of six in front of the boxes along the sides of the theatre, facing each other as they might in a church. The singing men stood behind them, and it was a moment before James realized what was odd. The youngest boy looked to be about nine. Three might have been between ten and twelve. Another four were about his own age or a little older, but the others had to be fifteen or sixteen. *And their voices hadn't changed yet.* Two were singing alto, and two treble.

James was so fascinated that he barely noticed when the psalm ended and the Master held up a hand for attention. He spoke of the importance of *Cynthia's Revels* as the first play to be presented at Queen Elizabeth's Court in the new century, and he began to read off the last few assignments of parts in Master Jonson's play. ". . . and the silent figures Phronesis, Thauma, and Time are Gerard Pocock, James Parrett, and Thomas Grimes. All of you but Parrett will go now to the tiring room, where Master Chelsum's tailors will see to the measurements for your costumes. Parrett, you will come with me."

A startled James followed the Master to a table near the stage where a middle-aged man in a neat black gown with a white collar sat, quietly fingering the keys on a pair of virginals. It was a larger version of the sort of tabletop piano that Phil had made. The soft notes stopped when the black-gowned man saw their approach.

"Dr. Bull," said the Master, "this is Parrett. Young Garland says that he can sing, but his speech is neither smooth nor clear, which is not promising. I would like to have him even if he is only passing good, but not if you can never use him for the choir. We will hear him together."

Dr. Bull gave James a quizzical look. "So, then. What will you sing, Parrett?"

James had decided, almost without thinking, that—like it or not—he needed to try his best. If he didn't, he could be out on the street in the middle of winter. Besides, if there were sixteen-year-olds whose voices hadn't changed, maybe he wasn't so peculiar after all. The difficulty was that he wasn't sure which of the old songs Reenie sang had been written yet—*weird thought!*—and so he hesitated.

"Very well." Dr. Bull nodded and turned to sort through the sheets of handwritten music on the table. "Here is the new setting for one of our poet's songs. I will play the first stanza through and then begin. Take the cantus part your first time through, and in the second we will try you at a descant while I play the cantus."

At James's blank look, Dr. Bull raised his eyebrows at the Master. "The descant, Parrett. The treble that dances above the line."

James knew what a descant was, and could only make a desperate stab at a guess that the "cantus" must mean the soprano, the treble line. He had time only to scan as far as the first chorus before Dr. Bull, at the virginals, returned to the opening bars. The handwriting was quite different from the poet's and easy enough to read, though some words James did not know. He wasn't even sure what they added up to, but he took a deep breath and jumped in.

> Queen and huntress, chaste and fair,
> Now the sun is laid to sleep,
> Seated in thy silver chair . . .

Except for the night on the moonlit hill above the City, James had not sung with his whole heart since the second grade. At first he was uncomfortably aware of the words and notes on the page and the two pairs of sharp eyes fixed on him, then these blurred into the patterns of color and line, light and shade in the great room. As the virginals' *tunk-tunky*, cherry-sweet toy-piano-like notes carried the melody, James's voice danced with it, growing stronger with each phrase until for him that melody was all there was. When he came to the third and last chorus—*"Thou that mak'st a day of night,/Goddess excellently bright"*—he found himself wanting to grin. The second time through, he sang a descant to the melody. Descanting was something he had often heard but never done, and he sang it with a deepening surprise that he *could*, and an even deeper surprise at his own pleasure.

The Master and Dr. Bull looked at each other and said nothing.

"And the psalm the Children were singing earlier?" the Master asked. "The cantus part."

Dr. Bull struck a chord, and James took a breath and sang, a little uncertainly at first because the words had been different from those he knew, but by "Approach with joy his courts unto," with growing confidence. Reenie and Phil would have been astonished to hear him, and equally amazed to discover that he could still remember any song he really listened to, just as when he was two he had parroted every new song he heard on *Sesame Street* or *Mister Rogers' Neighborhood*. James, amazed himself, finished the final verse with a shiver of relief.

The Master spoke first. "A pity." He tucked his chin down and raised his eyebrows as if he were asking a question.

Dr. Bull nodded. "Waste is always a pity. The lad's voice is sadly untrained. His pitch is faultless, but his breath uneven. You are right, but though we cannot turn a turnip into a pear between now and Friday, this seems more a matter of transmuting a pippin into a Sops-of-Wine before the sixth of January and Twelfth Night." He smiled. "An apple fit for a queen."

The Master's stern mouth glimmered briefly into a smile, and he nodded.

James's resentment at being talked about over his head rose again. They *seemed* to be saying that he hadn't sung them off their feet, but with their help he just might learn how to. Grandma used pippin apples for her cooking, so was "Sops-of-Wine" some special kind of apple? The thought of Grandma's apple crumble and apple pie and his own hunger made him feel suddenly light-headed.

"Parrett!"

Startled, James saw the Master's frown and tried to push down the sudden rush of panic that had swept over him. "Sir?"

"Attend, Parrett. I have no patience for day-dreamers. You are to go now, and to join the other boys in the tiring room. Master Chelsum, when he has measured you for your costume as Thauma, will do so for your Chapel coat."

Dr. Bull stood and gave James a light push toward the stage. "Go, child! Your complexion and the queen's scarlet will make a handsome show."

The tiring room—as in "attire," or clothing, James was told—was a large dressing and waiting room behind the stage. Costumes hung on racks of pegs along the walls, and at a table amid the benches and the jostling boys, a tailor was marking and pinning tucks to be taken in on colorful men's suits and women's gowns that were to be sent off to be cut down to boy size.

The small, gap-toothed tailor measured James and

passed him along to Master Chelsum. Master Chelsum had only one suit of the queen's livery, and when it turned out to be too large he gave orders that it be cut down and made to fit. "You will have it on the morrow, and the shirts and smallclothes that go with it," he promised, and paused. A small, puzzled frown furrowed his forehead. "Odd. We have just such a suit as you wear in our store here. The same color, same embroidery, same exact new-fashioned breeches. It would seem some one of our tailors sits up at night to sew for customers of his own. I must make sure he does not use our wool! But, go now! That is the bell for dinner."

James, going, shook his head in wonder. Plumed Hat had borrowed—or stolen—his suit from the tiring room of the Children of the Chapel Royal! But then—if his rescue from the river hadn't happened yet, was the suit still there? Could there *be* two suits in the same place and time? The thought made him distinctly nervous. He decided he didn't want to know.

"Dinner," it turned out, was lunch, and was set out on the long table in the first downstairs room. After a reading from the Bible by Mr. Sharpe, one of the Gentlemen of the Chapel, and a short blessing pronounced by the Master, the Children sat down on benches and stools to a meal of cold beef pie, cheese, wheat bread and butter, and beakers of thin beer. Even as he chewed and swallowed, James's feeling of the unreality of everything around him deepened. He had that eerie sense again of being separate from it all—of watching a brightly colored movie done in period costume.

After the meal the Master announced that the afternoon was to follow its regular pattern of rehearsal upstairs in the theatre and lessons in the schoolroom beyond the room where James and Thomas first were taken.

Lessons? James blinked and sat up straighter.

"Those who have not had a chance to learn their speeches will bring them when they are called. We will begin at the beginning and set places and movements on the stage. We will go briskly, so that all may return to their lessons before six of the clock. Tomorrow, the twelve who sing the Chapel services will be taken before the morning meal to Whitehall Palace. I have ordered the boats to be at Blackfriars stairs, ready to leave at seven. On your return after the service, two of the Gentlemen will accompany you— to assure that there is no fighting or swearing or playing at dice."

James leaned forward to try to see whom the Master was frowning at as he spoke, but could not tell. Every face was wide-eyed with a "Who, me, sir? Not I, sir!" look so familiar that he had to smother a laugh. At just that moment every head at the table suddenly bowed, and James turned to see that the Master had put the palms of his hands together. In a voice that was half solemn, half brisk, he gave thanks for the excellent cold pie they had just eaten and called down blessings on the lessons to come.

Except for the eleven who would be onstage in the play's prelude and first act, the boys made their way through to the schoolroom with pushing and shoving, laughter, and the "*Ow!*"s of stepped-on toes. James would have felt right at home, except that no one pushed *him* or stepped on his toes. The younger boys wriggled past the others to be close to James as they made their way to their places, and the older boys who glanced his way stared with a sharper curiosity as they settled on their stools. One small boy who reached his side looked up eagerly. "Do the savages in America *really* go naked?" he asked. James shook his head. "I didn't see any," he answered cautiously.

In the schoolroom, four tables held neatly arranged books and folded-paper notebooks, ink bottles and pens, five or six sets to a table. A portable podium sat atop a smaller table at the front of the room, near the fire. The teacher, who entered after the boys, was a mild-looking middle-aged man with yellowish skin, dark shadows under his eyes, and a dry cough. As he came in, the boys stood quickly, with a scraping back of stools, and said with one voice, "Good afternoon, Master Moult."

"Good afternoon." Mr. Moult coughed. The boys sat down. Mr. Moult coughed again and placed a small round object beside the books he had spread out on his table. He picked up a book and opened it to a page marked with a slip of paper. Then, with a pointer like an orchestra conductor's baton, he pointed at James's table.

"Field! *Discrutior animi, quia ab domo abeundum est mihi.*" James recognized the language easily enough as Latin because of Christmas carols like "*Adeste Fideles*" and some of the concert songs Reenie sang.

"Sir." Field, a slender, dark-haired boy with a pointed face, stood, swallowed nervously, and translated the line into an English sentence that earned him only a "Hmph! More graceful spoken than phrased, but well enough. Next—Baxter! *Tum omnes pariter ex sartiagine exilientes.*"

In quick succession Mr. Moult's pointer stabbed here and there around the tables, taking sentences from this book and that on his own table.

"Mottram!"

"Day!"

"Ostler!"

"Pykman!"

"Martin!"

"Grimes!"

James sat very still. That usually helped when he hadn't finished his social studies homework and Mr.

Everson was firing off questions. It worked now—or perhaps Mr. Moult enjoyed letting the new boys wait for the axe to fall. He hadn't called on Thomas or the three others, either.

At three o'clock, Mr. Moult looked at his small round table clock and closed his book. "Intermission," he announced. "The new boys will return in ten minutes so that I may judge their skill in Latin."

The boys shot to their feet and stood waiting while Mr. Moult took up his books and left. From a respectful silence, the room exploded into cheerful sound. A few boys bent over their books. One yawned and put his head down. A younger boy shouted, "Blindman's Buff! In the outer yard," and led a noisy gaggle out the door. James drifted along in the wake of the half dozen who headed for the privy.

James was last in line, and when he came out the other six boys had vanished back into the theatre building. The corridor was empty, and instead of going back along it to the first of the main building's large rooms, James took his chance and turned right, toward the door at the end of the hallway, and out. He found himself in an outdoor passage that led between the theatre and another outbuilding to a walkway that crossed it at right angles.

The second walkway ended at an arched door in a high wall. James was about to turn back when he heard a bump and a curse from the other side of the wall, and the arched door began to creak open. He darted out of sight around a corner.

The two men who came through carried heavy-looking wooden kegs on their shoulders. They went in at the corridor door James had come out of and closed it after themselves.

They had pushed the door in the wall shut.

But they had not fastened it.

eleven

JAMES MADE A DASH FOR THE DOOR.

Pulling it half shut behind him, he leaned out and found himself looking into a narrow lane.

To the right the lane climbed up between high walls toward a gateway he thought he had seen on the way from Ludgate down to the theatre. What could be better? To the left, the walled lane ran straight down to the river. Through the arch at its foot James could see the water, and a man carrying another wooden cask up a stair from a boat below. He placed it just inside the gateway with several of what from a distance looked like basketwork hampers. He then turned back to the stair.

James wanted to run, but as he stepped away from

the door, he forced himself to keep to a brisk walk. As he moved upward between the high stone walls, an uncomfortable tightness between his shoulders made him itch to look back, but he resisted. Along most of the way, upper windows in houses and great buildings overlooked the walls, and their stout doors and garden gates opened into the lane. From anywhere above, someone might look or step out and afterward be able to say, "A boy in brown? He went toward Ludgate." James wriggled his shoulders uncomfortably, as if he could feel the curious stares, and went on, up under a room built over the lane, and through an arched gateway. Then he did run. Turning left-right-left-right, he came out into Ludgate by the narrow passage along the side of the City gate itself. Once through the gate, he had only to retrace the way he and Thomas had been brought from Long Lane. *Was it only this morning?* he wondered wildly as he ran. Already it seemed an age ago.

He raced up Old Bailey past Newgate and into Gifford Street. He passed Pie Corner, where the aroma from cookshops banished for a few yards the smell of the streets' stiff mud. At one a stout black woman in an apron stood in the doorway, hands on hips, and called out, "Hot meat pies! My fine meat pies! Come, buy!" James almost stumbled in his surprise and dismay, for she looked like his sharp-tempered Aunt Deloreese to the life. But he ran on, and then he was in Smithfield. A bell tolled twice nearby, and he guessed it must be for half past three. In mid-December this far north, sunset ought to be—when? Some time around half-past four? He was going to have to wait in the church again. *Aunt Deloreese. Aunt Deloreese and Grandma* . . . He struggled to hold back tears.

The building site at Clerkenwell Close was bustling, and in the church James was met by the sound of young voices piping out what must have been a Bible verse: *"Where was thou when I laid the foundations of the earth? Declare, if thou hast understanding."* Toward the front of the church fifteen or twenty young children sat on benches facing an old gentleman in black. As James stood in the shadows beside the door, the old gentleman called on each child by name and commanded, "Verse five!" or

"Verse six!" The children stumbled through their verses, reading from the single small, fat Bible that passed awkwardly from hand to hand. No one paid attention as the heavy door clanked shut, so James moved quietly back to the bell tower room where he had waited before. The old cloak still hung on its peg. James was about to take it down, but remembered the warmer fleece and recovered it from its hiding place. Wrapped in it and tucked away in his shadowy corner, he was almost invisible.

Being invisible was a great relief. For a long, trembling moment all James could think was that for the first time since early morning no one was watching him. No curious eyes! He took a deep breath and let himself relax. Funny—

Suddenly it struck him that it *was* funny, and he had to fight the urge to give in to helpless giggles. Invisible? At home he seemed to swing from visible to invisible like a pendulum. On the street, in school, all he wanted to be was invisible, and usually he was. At home he never was. Everyone in his family, black and white, both sets of grandparents, and all the aunts and uncles and thirteen cousins crowded in on him, seeing themselves in him, expecting him to be like them, think like them, enjoy the same things, do the same things, pulling him one way and then the other. Even Reenie and Phil. The truth was, that was just another way of being invisible. *And he didn't want to be.* What he wanted was for them to see *him.* Him himself. More than just a part of themselves.

But then—James thought hard as he huddled against the cold. Maybe there wasn't a "him." He couldn't think of a single thing he did because he wanted to, or because he was interested. Until this morning . . .

Until he sang.

Sang.

From the way the Master and Dr. Bull looked at him, the way they spoke, he couldn't tell what they thought.

What mattered wasn't what they thought, though. It was what he felt, a feeling he remembered from when he was very small. The excitement of waking up in the mornings. The excitement of simply being awake . . . This morning in the theatre at Blackfriars he had actually tried his best. He sang his best and afterward knew there was a better "best" he didn't know how to reach. Even knowing that, he had felt as if . . . as if he were an electric light long ago plugged in, but never switched on. Maybe the expression "being taken out of yourself" meant more than being excited enough to forget your ordinary self. He had certainly been that in the last two days—in more ways than one.

But maybe being taken out of yourself could mean . . . being shown a self you weren't, but could be.

The buzz of thoughts fizzled out into vagueness as James's head nodded toward his knees.

When he awoke, the church was dark. The old man had left the key in the west door again, and when James turned it and stepped out, the night outside was almost as dark. He went slowly across the open space, feeling for each step among the frozen wheel ruts. As he went, he kept an eye on the shadow sitting by the watchman's fire back by the new construction.

The shimmer on the stairs had moved again, this time not sideways but up, so that it rested at the edge of the landing. The changes always made him uneasy, but this time at least it made going through easier, and the basement side looked safely dark, as always. All he had to do was drop to his hands and knees and crawl through. Once he had, and had felt his way to the steps and pulled the light cord, he went straight to the janitor's sink and reached up behind it.

The cloth-wrapped clock was not there.

James's heart *tick-tocked* loudly in his ears. Why wasn't it there? It had to be the caretaker. He must have found and taken it. James wavered between anger and alarm. It had seemed a perfect way to find out what day it was without going up to the flat and taking a chance on being seen. Now he had to go up.

At least, he saw with relief, it was daylight in his own time. Light spilled down the stairwell into the front hallway from the skylight far overhead. Feeling suddenly silly in his knee-length breeches and embroidered jerkin and makeshift fleece lap-robe cloak, James folded the lap robe and placed it on the top basement step. Out by the front door he spied the drift of letters and circulars that had been pushed through the front-door letter slot. Hurrying to scoop them up, he sat on the bottom stair step to leaf through them. The advertisements for estate agents and pizza delivery he sent spinning back to the floor by the door. The letters, all addressed to Charles Parrett, were mostly from businesses.

One was from Pittsburgh, in his father's handwriting.

The postmarks were all from the twenty-first of March of this year or earlier. *His* "this year." The one from his dad was postmarked *March 14*. March. The shimmer-circle's freakish way with time had brought him back more than two months too soon!

What was he to do? The mail came just before eight o'clock, so if Cousin Charles wasn't off at his house in Italy, he might be upstairs eating breakfast right now. James stood and let the letters drop into a little heap below the letter slot. He was calm as he walked back to the basement door, but calm or not, he found tears running down his cheeks. They didn't stop until he splashed his face with cold water at the janitor's sink and dried it on the cloth that hung there. Then he sat down on the steps to think.

Clearly, the clock was gone from the basement because he hadn't put it there yet. All that seemed clear about the skittery shimmers, though, was the obvious: that this one was *tied* to the Clerk's Well, and the other to the river. Remembering the tingle he had felt near Oxford Street on one of the expeditions with his father, he wondered whether there might be other shimmers too faint to show themselves, places where the present almost touched the past, but not quite. The more James thought about it, "his" portal did seem to stay roughly in the same place—the same *space*—but the two *times* it touched kept wobbling around. The shimmer was tricky.

In his imagination James tried to stretch the portal out between Now and Then. The first picture that came to him was a Slinky toy, which had two ends that could wobble around. When that didn't help, he tried to think of it in the shape of a tornado: not a *tornado* tornado, just its shape. There was a middle— the shimmer by the well—that held almost still while the top went wobbling around the present, and the bottom wobbled around in the past.

Which didn't help his own problem much.

If the portal was obeying rules, they were ones he didn't understand. There was no way he was going to be able to figure out when coming through to the basement would land him on the day he fell into the past. He would have to settle for any day between the day he and Reenie and Phil had arrived and the Millennium Bridge day—and hope for the best. It made no sense that two of him could exist at the same time. So if one of him winked out on the spot, so what? They were both him.

Except that it did matter.

I'm more ME than he is, James thought in sudden desperation. *I'm more me!*

And he had to get back. As quickly as he could.

The faintly seen stair on the other side of the shimmer was no longer dark.

James had been so swallowed up in his thoughts that he hadn't noticed any change or movement. When he pulled the light cord and turned back toward the portal, he was startled to see shadows stir in it and then resolve themselves into legs: the legs of a man moving down the stair. James could make out, strapped onto his back, a tall, pitcher-shaped wooden vessel made of shaped slats bound together with twisted willow hoops, like a barrel. James kept well back, and watched nervously until the man climbed back into sight.

As he did, he moved heavily under the awkward weight of the great wooden pitcher, which sloshed water at every upward step. He was watching his footing carefully, but even as his lower body and then his legs moved through the circle in the air in a grisly cross-section of flesh and bone—*gross!*—and vanished, there was no sign that the man saw even a glimmer of the opening.

Wild with impatience, James stepped around to the other side of the shimmer to watch the water carrier on his climb up to the Close. He had waited far too long already. If he were to wait any longer he might arrive back in the past days before, or days after, he had come through, even such a little time ago. He couldn't go up to the church with workmen there, but there was no reason he couldn't go down and out by way of the well. He was about to crawl through to the landing when he remembered the fleece lap robe. He retrieved it from the top basement step, dithered for a moment, and then gave a snort at his own slow-wittedness. He didn't have to go *up* to the church to return it to its hiding place in the church, just down to the well and up around the corner.

Five minutes later, the gray fleece was tucked behind its battered angel.

The teacher and small children, once again struggling through the Book of Job, did not notice as James slipped in and out. He angled across the green and took off down Turnmill Street as fast as he could run. By the time he made his way down through the City to the great arch of Ludgate and turned to make his way down toward Water Lane, he was out of breath and had a painful stitch in his side. At least, he told himself as he ran, he had stopped feeling cold.

The door in the wall along Water Lane that led to the back entrance to the Blackfriars theatre was still—or again—ajar. James reached out a hand to ease it open, but before he touched it the door was snatched inward and a boy in the crimson coat of the Chapel Children burst out and crashed straight into him. When James saw that it was Jack Garland, the boy from Long Lane and the morning ambush, he jumped back.

"Oh—you!"

Jack looked even more startled than James, and more flustered. "I was looking for you," he said quickly. "Mr. Moult has asked for you—and I am to tell you we are not to go abroad without leave. And then only in twos. Where were you?"

James blinked. If it was still intermission, he must have come back almost as soon as he had left.

twelve

MR. MOULT SAT AT THE LONG TABLE IN THE MIDDLE great room with Thomas and the two other new boys, Walter Bassocke and Launcelot Gedge, perched on stools lined up in front of him. When he saw James, he pointed at a fourth stool, then turned his attention back to Thomas. "I have no wish to beat you, Clifton. I repeat: Continue with the translation. *Sequitur, ut hæc officiorum genera persequar . . .*"

Thomas's shoulders drooped in defeat. "It remains now that I treat that sort of duty," he answered almost too softly to be heard.

"Thank you, Clifton. And you, Parrett, continuing from *De Officiis: quæ pertinent ad vita cultum, et ad earum rerum, quibus vituntur homines facultatem. . . .*"

James shifted uncomfortably on the stool. "I can't—sir."

"Cannot, Parrett?" Mr. Moult folded his hands and looked up at the heavy beams on the ceiling. "Or will not?"

"Can't," James said. He wasn't sure how much to explain. The less the better, he guessed. "My school didn't teach Latin."

As he spoke, out of the corner of his eye James caught a flicker of crimson behind the half-open door to the outer room. Garland. Two to one it was Garland. He hadn't come in, but he hadn't gone away, either.

"No Latin!" Mr. Moult was shocked. "What school teaches no Latin? An academy for ratcatchers and refuse collectors? A dame school for infants?"

"I can speak Italian, a little," James offered quickly. "My parents sent me for lessons every week. Because there are so many good songs in Italian, I guess."

"Mmph! Then you at least will be able to converse with Signor Bonetti, the dancing master," Mr. Moult replied sourly. He shook his head unhappily. "The Master will not like this. Not at all." He sighed and looked at Thomas and the other three. "For the morrow the four of you will translate into English Erasmus's colloquy on 'Things and Names,' and write it out in a fair hand. For now, you may go along to the schoolroom and your French lessons with Mr. Porteous."

As Mr. Moult rose, church bells nearby tolled the half hour—the end of intermission—and he paused with his hand on the door. "First, Bassocke, you will slip up to the theatre and tell the Master—" He frowned and suddenly pulled the door open. "Ho, sirrah! Skulking behind doors?"

Jack Garland barely caught himself as he stumbled into the room.

"Garland?" The disapproval on Mr. Moult's thin face wavered and settled itself into mildness. "I did not mean to startle you so. As it happens, you come at the pinch. I was about to send Bassocke here to tell the Master I must speak with him on a matter of importance, but you will know better where to find him if he is not above."

James saw young Garland's hard-eyed flare of anger transform itself so swiftly to a pale blankness and then an eager innocence that he wasn't sure he hadn't imagined it.

"Yes, sir," Garland said, and vanished.

"Parrett?"

James jumped a little. "Yes, sir."

Mr. Moult took a deep breath. "Here—here are your Latin grammar and Erasmus's *Colloquies*. Begin by reading the grammar on nouns and adjectives, and memorizing the five declensions of nouns. I will set exercises for you tomorrow," he added before bustling out.

James took the books to his place at the second table in the schoolroom with a sinking feeling. He hadn't counted on *work*. Italian wasn't so bad. People spoke Italian. But—a *dead* language? He took a quick look into Lily's *Latin Grammar* and almost groaned. Even though he didn't understand a word of it, the Latin looked easier to read than the English. The Latin at least was in ordinary letters; the English, for some reason, was printed in 𝔭𝔯𝔦𝔠𝔨𝔩𝔶 𝔟𝔩𝔞𝔠𝔨 𝔩𝔢𝔱𝔱𝔢𝔯𝔰 that clumped together on the page.

The boys and the French master, Mr. Porteous, came in, and the last of the Children were settling into their places in the schoolroom when they heard the Master's and others' voices raised in the next room. Mr. Porteous, startled, hurried out of the room and closed the door after him. Before it thumped shut, the boys heard the Master exclaim, "Are you sure?"

After that, all they could hear were murmurs. Little Trussell tiptoed up and put his ear to the heavy oak door, but it was only to roll his eyes, shrug his shoulders, and return to his stool.

A new murmur joined the others outside.

"The bricklayer," Garland announced in a stage whisper. He rose from his seat to stalk to the front of the room and back in an exaggerated imitation of the poet Jonson's ungainly gait.

"What does he mean, 'bricklayer'?" Thomas breathed.

The boy named Baxter leaned close to answer. "Garland says when poetry cannot feed his family Mr. Jonson works as a laborer."

James frowned. "Jack Garland? How would he know?"

"Garland's brother is a player, and knows him well. But take care never to speak of it. Our poet is a good enough fellow, but he can go off like gunpowder!"

The door opened and the room fell silent. The Master entered first, and the boys stood so quickly that two stools fell over. "Good afternoon, Master."

The Master gave a brief nod. "Good afternoon. Act Four, please. Upstairs. The rest of you will go on with your lesson until called."

The crimson-coated boys of Act Four lined up by twos and left the room with a cocky flourish. The corner of the Master's mouth gave a twitch that might have been a smile.

"Mr. Porteous, the others are yours, but for Parrett. Parrett will come with me."

James, half worried because he didn't know what was up, and half relieved to be away from the class, followed the Master into the middle room, where Benjamin Jonson stalked up and down. A servant was at the fireplace, laying a new fire on top of the dying coals of the morning's fire. When Jonson saw James, he hurried across the room to place a hand on his shoulder.

The Master turned to the servant. "Go find Dr. Bull, Gowthrop. I think he has not left yet."

Jonson cocked his head at James. "Is it true what Mr.

Moult tells us, lad?" he demanded. "No scrap of Latin? Not a *quo* or *quis* or *quid*? If your father is a teacher of music, he is educated. Did he not mean you to rise to his station in life because your mother is African?" The poet was indignant. "It is shameful if he did not!"

James drew back, startled and angry, and puzzled too.

The poet lowered his voice and spoke more gently. "You need not worry yet, James Parrett."

The Master interrupted. "What Mr. Jonson means, young Parrett, is that we may be able to keep you, and we may not. The queen wishes her Chapel servants to be well educated, but the purse she gives me is not so fat that I can furnish the extra lessons you will need unless Dr. Bull and I judge you worth it. There would be Latin, and singing, and instruments. A singer should know the lute at the very least. And perhaps we will have you taught to dance."

"Pfah!" Mr. Jonson snorted. "Dancing! I would as lief there were no dances in plays. They do not mirror nature. They . . ."

Gowthrop stuck his head back in at the door, putting an end to the poet's grumble. "Dr. Bull was just leaving for Gresham's College, sir. He is coming in at the Great Yard door now."

"I do not wish to delay him. I will speak to him in the entry," the Master said, and swept out the door.

James's throat tightened. If the Master decided not to keep him, how was he going to survive—to *eat*—in this dazzling, filthy, fascinating, and terrifying all-white world where he stood out like a palm tree in a pear orchard? His stomach growled. How *would* he eat?

Mr. Jonson lumbered to the door. "I must leave you, Parrett. I am needed above. The Master has trusted the setting-out of the movements on stage to his son-in-law, but Robinson does not know his trap-door from his arras."

"Sir?" James darted after the poet. "Sir, I don't understand. Does the Master want to keep me? Why would he, if it's so much trouble? I want to stay, but—why?"

Jonson's eyebrows shot up and he gave a snort of laughter. "Why? Bless you, lad, he seems to believe that silver dollars drop from your mouth when you sing. My ears are not so well-tuned as his. I cannot judge how much of it is your warbling and how much the color of your skin, but indeed, yes. He does wish to keep you."

"Sir?" James asked warily. "The old king's black—his African trumpeter that Mr. Giles talked about, and the queen's dancers. Was he—are they slaves?"

"John Blanke a slave? No, never!" The poet gave James a look that said, *Is that what frights you?* and shook his head violently. "This is a kingdom of free men, and any slave whose foot touches English earth is in the instant free. Do not fret thee over *that*, dear child." He looked faintly uncomfortable as he said it, and gave James's shoulder a clumsy parting pat. But then, with his hand almost on the door latch, he turned and came lumbering back. "Still, you'd best take care among strangers, lad," he said. "That may be the old heart of the law, but there are folk with sour hearts and pinched minds who hate foreigners. Four or five years ago some such complained to the queen that there were too many blackamoors in England and prayed her to send them out of it."

James felt uneasy at the poet's scowl. "What did she do?"

"Why, made a proclamation ordering that every

African should be sent out of the kingdom."

"But—" James was confused.

Mr. Jonson shrugged. "The queen does what is politic. Her officers ordered a dozen or so London folk to send their African servants onto a German ship in the Thames, and after it sailed no more was heard of the proclamation—or of the hundreds of blacks left safe behind."

James saw a shadow pass across the poet's face.

"Did something—what happened to the servants?" James asked.

"Why, what do you think? The German captain sold them for slaves. So my advice to you, young Parrett, is to be wary of sour faces and seafarers." He opened the door and was gone.

Left alone in the still-chilly room, James tried to digest a definition of freedom that allowed the Master or the queen to snap up boys or Africans willy-nilly. Being cold didn't help. He rubbed his hands together for warmth, and then tried tucking them into his armpits. No one else seemed much bothered by the next-to-unheated rooms. If he was so spoiled by having had central heating in wintertime, how long was it going to take to get used to the cold?

Silver dollars? Mr. Jonson had said "silver dollars." That couldn't be right, could it? Did they have dollars, too? And—what *about* his color? James scowled and kicked at a massive leg on the long dining table.

The door opened and the Master reentered.

"Dr. Bull is our organist, Parrett, and a doctor of music. He and I agree that you must stay. However, the Children's lodgings with Mistress Matcham in Knightrider Street are crowded to overflowing. She has said that until the new rooms she is adding are ready, she can take no more. I will make arrangements for one of the teaching masters or singing men to house you, and for masters to instruct you. You may return now to the classroom. I will speak with you later."

"But, sir—"

"*Now*, Parrett."

James was almost as relieved as he was famished. At least, now he could last until the next chance he got to try to reach Clerkenwell—Cousin Charles's Clerkenwell.

I will get home. . . .

The last nine boys in class, whose characters were not on stage until Act Five of Mr. Jonson's play, were not called upstairs until after four-thirty.

James, watching while he waited for his own entrance as Thauma, could not sort out who was who among the twenty-three or -four characters, or what most of their wordy speeches meant, but he was fascinated. The older boys played men with fancy names like Crites or Anaides or Amorphus. The younger ones played women with names like Phantaste or Argurion. They reeled off long speeches with a lordly air, but once in a while James had to blink at some of the words that whizzed by him. The pace was so quick that he couldn't be sure whether they were dirty or not. Snickers from the Children waiting to go on made him suppose they were at least rude or crude.

Mr. Jonson at one point explained to James that the name of his own character, Thauma, meant "miracle." Mr. Jonson clearly liked his actors, but he could bellow like a bull if a word was dropped. He shouted that the musicians were out of tune. He swore at a wardrobe man for not getting off the stage when told. He sat with his head in his hands and moaned as the new boy Gedge read the Jeweler's lines. He put an arm around Chappell when he blubbered after being whipped for spilling ink on his Latin grammar book. And then he roared out, "Property Master, where in Creation are Cupid's bow and arrows?" James decided that the real miracle about playing Miracle was that Thauma had no speeches to earn a howl from the poet.

Listening to Mr. Jonson's play, James wasn't sure, but the idea seemed to be that with understanding and time and miracles, the eight foolish men and women who were Cynthia's courtiers would learn to be "real" and serve their queen as they ought to. It was a sermon, he decided: a weird, wordy, frothy sermon with songs.

The blocking rehearsal was finished at six. The boys trooped down the great winding stair, collected their schoolbooks, and lined up two by two to walk to their lodgings and Mistress Matcham's supper table in nearby Knightrider Street. Only Garland hung back.

"Parrett. Clifton." Mr. Evans beckoned them out of the line. "Parrett, the Master has arranged with Mr.

Moult to house and board you and Clifton. Mr. Moult will also tutor you in Latin and rhetoric. He has room for three, and so Garland has offered to go in place of another of the new boys. I have seen to the purchase of beds and bedding, and the tailors will have your new clothing ready on the morrow. Buswell will go with your coach and the cart. Now, follow me."

Garland again. James slid a quick, mistrustful glance in Jack's direction. The boy's narrow, high-cheeked face was handsome, but he had a watchful, heavy-lidded look odd on a ten- or eleven-year-old, and he seemed to lurk around every corner. If it hadn't been Garland who had set up Thomas, and James himself, to be snatched, James would have shrugged and ignored him. But what was it he had said so eagerly to the Thomas-snatchers? *"Take the African."* That the Master would be sure to take him *"when he has heard this parrot sing."*

James had an odd, uneasy feeling that something more lay behind that eagerness than one verse of "When that I was a little tiny boy."

But what else could there be?

thirteen

THE COACH, WITH A CART CREAKING IN ITS WAKE, rumbled past the great bulk of St. Paul's Cathedral in the winter darkness, the servant Buswell walking ahead with a lantern. The streets were lit here and there along the way by the yellowish glow of lamps hung beside doorways, but the darkness swallowed up their glimmer almost before it touched the street. In the darkest stretches Buswell went more slowly, and the boys could hear the driver mutter about householders who defied the law and refused to hang out lamps. At least the ruts frozen in place after the last rain had thawed a little and been pounded down enough by feet and hooves and wheels, so that the ride was a bit smoother than James's rocky coach ride with Plumed Hat and the stout gentleman.

Not one of the three boys spoke. Thomas huddled in a corner. Jack Garland stared into the outer darkness with narrowed eyes, busy in some world or secret of his own. James, reminded of the afternoon of his rescue from the river, and of the tavern and the coach ride, decided that the first day was far colder. Yes, he had been half frozen from his plunge into the river, and now he was snug in a new warm cloak of felted wool and wearing warm woolen gloves, but this afternoon he had made his way to the Clerk's Well without a cloak, and that first time he had been freezing, cloak or no. If that earlier dip into this time had in fact happened *later*, in the deep of January or February, it would explain Plumed Hat's not knowing him.

At the pinnacled water-conduit house where the stout gentleman's coach had turned left, Buswell led the coach to the right along a wide street bordered along both sides for as far as James could see by splendid houses three and a half storeys tall. All had shuttered-up shops on the ground floor, and the dwellings in the storeys above made a glowing golden avenue of diamond-paned windows lit by lantern and candlelight.

"Whoo! What street is this?"

"Cheapside," Thomas answered distantly. "Goldsmiths and other rich shops."

At the next corner, the coach horses turned left out of Cheapside, following Buswell and his lantern. They passed a square-towered church, and James looked from one side to another, watching for other landmarks to remember. "And what street's this?"

Thomas gave an "I don't know" shrug.

Garland flicked a look in James's direction that James could not read. "Forster Lane," he said.

Near its end, narrow Forster Lane passed under a room that had been built between the upper storeys of two large old facing houses. Beyond that came a lane Garland said was Noble Street and, along its curve, a left turn into Mugwell Street.

"Mugwell Street?"

Garland spoke in an uncanny imitation of Mr. Moult's dry, singsong teaching voice. "Ah, interesting name, Parrett. Mugwell Street. Also known as Muggle Street. Properly, it should be Monkwell or Monkswell

Street, a name taken from the old well in the grounds of St. James's Hermitage near Cripplegate."

Garland's imitation roused a halfhearted giggle from Thomas, who had grown more and more miserable as the day wore on with no sign of his father's promised return. James managed a weak grin, but his mind had drifted unhappily to another old well.

At the top of Mugwell Street the coach drew up before the next-to-last house on the left. The lamp hanging outside the door showed little more of the house than its dark oak doorposts and the lintel beam above carved with acorns and the date 1547. From the height of the roofline dark against the starry sky it looked no more than two storeys high, with a loft or attic above. A red-cheeked Mrs. Moult opened the door to them.

"Oh, 'tis the young gentlemen already! Step in, and I will send Georgie over to the school for Mr. Moult." With one hand she held the door open, and with the other kept a firm hold on the collar of a small, even redder-cheeked girl who clapped her hands and cried, "Horsie! Want to see horsie!"

"No, Alice. The horse does not wish to see thee. It only wishes to go home as soon as the men unload the cart. Now, come."

"School?" James whispered to Jack Garland. "What does she mean, 'the school'?"

"Old Moult teaches Latin to the second-years at Mr. Speght's school next door for the extra fees. He thinks the Master and Mr. Evans know nothing of it." Garland's grin made James wonder whether he might have been a little bird that told the Master.

Young Georgie was quickly sent for his father. Buswell and the carter unloaded the cart and carried the bed-frame parts and bundles of bedding into the front room. A moment later Mr. Moult appeared from the school next door.

"Good evening, Clifton. Parrett. Garland. Come through, Buswell. The stair is just inside the kitchen. My children's beds have been moved to the garret for now, so you may leave all this in the room at the top of the stair. The servants will see to it."

When Buswell, coach, and cart were gone and the door was closed against the cold, Mrs. Moult urged the boys out of the chilly parlor—which had no fireplace—and into the kitchen. The table there was set for supper with spoons and knives, trenchers—flat pieces of wood hollowed out for plates—a platter with a roast of pork, dishes with buttered parsnips and brown bread and cheese, and an apple pie. Mr. Moult bowed his head and spoke a grace over the food—an agreeably short one compared with the Master's long blessing of the noon meal. Afterward, everyone sat down, the boys and children on stools, and Mr. Moult on a chair from the parlor. Mrs. Moult brought a pitcher of ale and another of milk, then upended a large basket and sat on it at the foot of the table.

Everyone ate in silence. No one spoke more than a word or two. Overhead, bumps and creaks and footsteps sounded until an old manservant and a little maidservant came down and sat by the fire to wait. When the pie was almost finished, Mr. Moult cleared his throat, and the little maidservant set to clearing the table. When she had done, she and the old man settled down in the fireplace corner to finish off the roast and pie. Mr. Moult looked around and rubbed his hands together with what seemed more anxiety than pleasure.

"How pleasant it is to have a full house!" he said.

After an awkward moment—while Jack Garland smothered a smile—Mrs. Moult jumped into the silence. "Shall we have us a song? Georgie, fetch the music, and Nell, your lute and mine. Let us try a catch to start."

Everyone rose to lend a hand. Three more stumpy wooden candlesticks were brought, and short candle ends found. One out of a dozen or so large, folded sheets of paper was chosen and spread out in the center of the table and weighted down by the candlesticks at its corners, and the candles lit. James leaned over and saw that the words and music for the three parts, cantus, altus, and bassus, were printed on the single sheet facing three different ways so that they could be read by the singers around a family table. Mrs. Moult and silent Nell, who was about fifteen, tuned their lutes.

A "catch" turned out to be what James would have called a "round," and the first was "Sleep, O Sleep,

Fond Fancy." Mr. Moult sang out with a booming bass and Mrs. Moult a fine alto. Shy Nell's was too soft to hold its own, but she made up for it on the lute. Small Alice piped up when she knew the words, and the old man followed the alto part in a thin, sweet counter-tenor. James, Jack, and Thomas, on the soprano side of the table, tried not to run over them all. Young Georgie had a tin ear, and more than once was warned by his father's frown not to bellow.

In what seemed no time at all, the candles had burned down to an inch and the fire in the great fire-place to ashes. Mr. Moult sent Georgie, Alice, and Nell up to the garret at the top and bed. Mrs. Moult followed, showing the boys into the bedroom above the kitchen. The three narrow beds had been set up and made up, and there were pegs for their clothes, and a chamber pot. Mr. Moult, explained when he came up that the "office of convenience," as he named it, was at the end of the garden, but the servants now slept in the little room above it, so chamber pots were provided for the nighttime.

"We go early to bed, I fear, for we must rise at six

to be at Blackfriars by seven." He used his bit of candle to light a small rush light in a lamp by the door. "Do not forget to say your prayers and to blow the light out," he warned as he entered into the front bedroom.

James was so tired that, when he sat down on the low middle bed, neither the rustle of straw in the new mattress nor the sound of weeping from Thomas could keep him from sleep. He barely managed to pull the blankets over his shoulders before he was gone.

At some time before midnight the cold awakened him. For a while he tried to ignore it, but bit by bit the chill and shivers crept inward until he felt the trembling creep beneath his breastbone. He forced himself out from under the blankets and up, to reach down his coat and cloak from their peg and spread them on top of his blankets. Only after he slipped back under did it seem to him that he had not seen Garland in his bed. Or had he?

James raised up blearily. The rectangle of faint light that fell in at the window lay across Jack Garland's bed, and the bed truly was empty. Where could he be? What was he—

But James was too exhausted to care. He flopped back down and tumbled into sleep.

In the dark of Tuesday morning, Jack Garland came to the kitchen table with the others, knuckling sleep from his eyes. Once the family and servants were gathered, Mr. Moult delivered himself of an earnest prayer of thanks for the new day and for the buttermilk and toasted bread the boys were eyeing hungrily through their eyelashes.

"Just a sip and a bite to hold you 'til your breakfast at Blackfriars," Mrs. Moult said to explain the smallness of the portions.

The coach collected Mr. Moult and the boys promptly, and before long they were warming their hands and backsides at the new fire in the middle room—the "refectory," as Mr. Moult called it—before the other Children arrived from their lodgings in Knightrider Street. James turned around and around in the warmth like a cook turning an underdone roast on a spit. Garland yawned. Thomas, who had been pale and silent, suddenly startled the room by announcing loudly, "My father *will* come today. He will!"

"God willing, he shall," Mr. Moult murmured quietly, so that only Thomas and James heard.

At seven o'clock in the classroom, the Master greeted the Children and led them in morning prayers and a long, depressing reading from a sermon by a Dr. Walter Chesterford. Afterward the room was silent for half an hour, except for the scratching of pens as the boys worked on the Latin compositions assigned the day before. James brought smothered laughter when he dipped his new goose quill directly into the inkwell. Jack Frost, an older boy sitting next to him, had to show him how to use a knife to trim the quill end into a pen point. As he finished, Frost leaned close to whisper, "Take care with your housemate Garland. Do not trust him overmuch. He is Evans's sneak."

"Who *is* Mr. Evans?" James whispered back. The short, stout Evans seemed to be everywhere, but rarely spoke to anyone but the Master.

"The Master's partner, the Gentlemen say. And chief penny-pincher. He keeps the purse and accounts."

A little before eight, the boys were served an early breakfast of milk, and oatmeal with butter. Then they were bundled into coaches and driven to the Revels offices in what once was St. John's Priory. There Edmund Tilney, the Master of the Queen's Revels, provided rehearsal rooms, and the Yeoman of the Revels oversaw wardrobe and tailoring rooms, and property and carpentry workshops. In an upper room the Children settled down to rehearsing, and those who had sung the early morning church service at the Chapel Royal in Whitehall Palace arrived at the end of morning intermission to join them. The play seemed far different from what James had seen of it the day before in the Blackfriars theatre. The scenes moved swiftly, and he had to blink at the boys' quickness and crispness of speech and the polish and ease of their acting. Even so, Mr. Jonson was everywhere, shouting, praising, tapping out a faster pace, raging at the unfortunate boy who tripped over a stool, and stooping to whisper gently and offer a handkerchief to one who got a bit of grit in his eye. The rehearsal carried on around him. James began to realize that

Cynthia's Revels was no school play. The Children were real play-actors, not children playing at acting.

James and Thomas were in the wardrobe workshop, trying on their new crimson coats and blue breeches sent from Westminster for fitting, when the uproar started. On the way back to the rehearsal hall they heard the room go silent except for two loud voices.

"'Tis my father!" Thomas crowed.

Shrugging off his bright new coat, Thomas thrust it at James and tore up the stair and into the rehearsal room. When James arrived, the boys were crowded close behind Mr. Evans, Mr. Robinson, Dr. Bull, and Gowthrop, who kept motioning them back. James slipped around to join them and watch the Master sputter in fury as a man whom the boys whispered was a court officer read aloud from a document with a large red seal.

"Clifton's father has won!" the boys whispered. *"No one has won against the Master before!"*

". . . for the release from Her Majesty's service of one Thomas Clifton, son to Henry Clifton, Esquire, of Toftrees in the County of Norfolk."

"Nonsense!" the Master flared. "By whose order?"

"By order of the Queen's Council," replied the officer. "The writ is signed by Sir John Fortescue, Chancellor of the Exchequer."

Thomas stepped to his father's side. With the same plain dignity as his father's, he gave the Master a nod of a bow and stalked after his father to the door. The officer made a deep bow and followed. James was a little disappointed—it was a victory that deserved more drama, at least a hug or a squeeze of hands if not outstretched arms and shouts of joy. He was suddenly desperate for his own parents. He found he could not swallow. *If* his *dad walked into the Revels rehearsal room with a writ, he would . . . well, to be honest, he wasn't sure what he* would *do.* At least he hoped he wouldn't stand there like a block of wood.

He trembled with a sudden shiver.

He had not once all morning thought about Reenie or Phil, or home, or slipping away to Clerkenwell Close. . . .

fourteen

JAMES HAD NO CHANCE ALL THAT DAY OR FOR THE
rest of the week to make his way back to the Clerk's
Well. Waiting was doubly hard because St. John's
was in Clerkenwell, and Clerkenwell Close had to be
nearby. Both, he knew, were north of Smithfield.
Beyond St. John's gate lay a great courtyard bordered
by the old monastery's buildings and walls, which, with
its gardens and grounds, were surrounded by an even
higher wall. James had a sick feeling that the church
tower visible just over the priory wall must belong to
St. James's Church across Clerkenwell Green. There
might even be a gate through to the green in the far
wall, but with one of the masters or Gentlemen always
at his elbow, he had no chance to find out.

On Wednesday, Dr. Bull came from Whitehall soon after nine o'clock. With him, he brought Edmund Browne, one of the Chapel Gentlemen, a "singing man," to teach James what he did badly when he sang, and how not to do it. Mr. Browne was also to rehearse James in a song for the last of the entertainments presented between the acts of the play. The Master and Mr. Evans led the three of them into a smaller rehearsal room.

"Here, Parrett." The Master held out a sheet of paper. "'Tis a new song I have composed to make a more fitting close to the final interlude than what we have now. You are to sing the cantus, and Mr. Browne will accompany you."

James looked at the paper to skim through the words as Mr. Browne took up his lute to play a stanza. The song's name was "Fair Cynthia, Rise," and the music and words were scored and lettered in the Master's neat, precise hand. James didn't think the poem was very good. The Master should have asked Mr. Jonson to write one. As Mr. Browne began again, he took a breath and sang.

Fair Cynthia, rise, our silver queen,
To deck our skies now darkly seen.
Thy glorious rays are all that light
And lead us safely through
The dreaming fields and streams of night.
Fair Cynthia, rise and grace our eyes,
Fair Cynthia, England's pearl of price.

Dr. Bull and the Master, with Mr. Evans, who popped in and out, spent half an hour listening to James singing "Fair Cynthia" for Mr. Browne. It seemed to James that the Master and Evans more than once exchanged sharp-eyed glances, but they said nothing more at the end than, "Well done, Parrett."

"Off with you, now," the Master added. "Down the stairs to Mr. Forshaw. His tailors have the Thauma costume all but ready, and must make sure of the fit."

"And you, Browne," Dr. Bull said cheerfully, "when you are content with our black canary's song, I will come hear him again."

Black canary? James frowned, not sure whether it was their private joke or a diss or a compliment. He went out to the stairs, but before he was out of earshot he heard the Master say, consideringly, "Black Canary . . ."

Mr. Evans's hard-edged voice cut in, "A find indeed! Can we put him before the playgoers on Saturday?"

Dr. Bull's murmur of "Too soon, too soon," was the last that James could hear.

"Parrett?" The costume master cocked his head and flicked through the tags on the garments hanging on one of the rails marked *Cynthia's Revels*. "Parrett. I mis-remember me. Is it Thauma or Time you're to have?"

"Thauma." James was glad he wasn't Time. That would be too weird for words. He gave a bitter little snort. *Time* was too weird for words.

While Mr. Forshaw went with one of the tailors to look for the costume, James crossed to the rear wall of the long wardrobe hall for a closer look at the scores of masks that hung there. Among the elegant, vacant-eyed faces and exaggerated comic ones, he was surprised to see three that were black. One was stylized and handsome, the second fairly realistic, but the third was unpleasantly cartoonish. Hanging beside it was a frizz of black wool that was its wig, and a pair of black gloves long enough to reach up to a man's shoulders. James was puzzled. Black gloves? Instead of makeup? Clearly there were *plays* with African characters, but he hadn't seen half a dozen Africans since he fell into this world, or time. . . .

Mr. Forshaw's voice startled him. "Parrett? Where *is* the lad?"

"Here, sir!"

James almost laughed out loud when he saw what he was to wear. He had already figured out that Thauma—Miracle—was female. He had learned that boys always took the women's parts in plays, that "players," as actors were called, were always men—and that there were no girls or women who were play-ers. It had not occurred to him that he would end up looking like—*this*. The white gown they were dressing him in was fantastical, with tiny mirrors set in the fabric, and a tall, winglike fan of a collar made of feathers tipped with pearls. For James, though, it was the shoes and the headdress that took the cake. The shoes, knee-high laced boots not meant to be seen, had soles ten inches high. Between them and the masked headdress topped with ostrich plumes, he had to look almost seven feet tall.

Mr. Forshaw rapped James's hand with a measuring stick. "Do not laugh, Parrett. Come, we will take off the headdress and gown. Then you must practice walking in the buskins. Thauma and her companions are to tower over the mere mortals, not totter. You may wear these up to your rehearsal, but I must have them again before you return to Blackfriars."

The rehearsal was finished a little before noon, so that James and Mr. Browne had time to go to St. Paul's to buy the songbooks he would need for his lessons. To James's amazement the cathedral grounds were filled up by tall, narrow houses on all sides but the front, and the ground floor of each house was a bookshop. Trestle-table stalls in front of each shop held new or sale-priced books, or old favorites. Each shop front showed its emblem on a painted sign: the Bishop's Head and the Angel displayed Bibles and books of sermons, others specialized in romances and adventures, or schoolbooks, or music.

There were signs for the Mermaid, the Blazing Stars, the Green Dragon, the White Horse, and the Tiger's Head. And, curiously, there was a sign for the Black Boy— although no black boy, or man, was to be seen. Some sold only books they themselves published, others sold volumes from Holland or France, Germany or Italy. At each, an apprentice boy manned the outdoor table and did his best to snare customers. "New today, sir! Tales of the Barbary pirates, just come from the press, sir!" or "A new ballad, sir! 'The Hanging of Roger Ratcliffe.' Come, buy!"

Idly James opened a volume with the title *A Blast Against the Theatres* on a table bearing a NEW THIS WEEK sign, and was caught by the date on the title page: 1600.

1600.

He was trying to digest this when suddenly, out of the corner of his eye, he caught sight of a familiar hat on a man riffling through the pages of a book at the next shop. *Velvet, with a green plume.* It was Plumed Hat! Quickly, James turned to Mr. Browne. "Sir?"

Mr. Browne looked up from a copy of Thomas Morley's *The Pleasure of Singing.* "What is it, Parrett?"

"That man at the next shop. Do you know who he is?"

Mr. Browne looked over James's head. "Which one?"

"The one in the green cloak, with the hat with the plume."

"That? Why, 'tis Tom Garland, young Garland's brother. He's a player with the Admiral's Men at the Fortune Theatre. Beyond Cripplegate. Ah, here we are, Parrett." Mr. Browne moved to the next stall, where there were neat stacks of song collections, music for the lute, and sheet versions of new ballads and popular catches.

"You will need Mr. Dowland's new book of songs and airs, and Mr. Morley's *Plain and Easy Introduction to Practical Music*, and Mr. Munday's lute songs." Mr. Browne handed the books to James, who was watching Plumed Hat Garland out of sight, and paid the bookseller with coins from the purse that hung at his waist.

"Now for our dinner," he said.

A noisy bustle to and from the kitchen in the addition along the west side of the building announced that dinner was already on the table in the refectory. The Master frowned at the latecomers, but after Mr. Browne bowed his head and said a silent grace, he said only, "Pass the pie to Mr. Browne if you will, Pavy."

After the pork pie, bread and butter, and weak beer, Mr. Browne led James back through the first large room—the "Blind Room" the boys called it, because it was so poorly lit by its one window—and out into the hallway that led past the kitchen. In the chamber next to the kitchen, a small-to-middling-size room, the cupboards along one wall held an impressive collection of musical instruments. Mr. Browne chose a six-string lute and handed it to James with a smile. "First lute lesson."

The feel under his hands of the beautiful half-of-a-pear shape of the body of the instrument, with its delicate parchment pierce-work rosette on the front, gave James a sharp pang.

Reenie, accompanying herself on the lute as she sang . . .

His dad, smoothing one last, thin coat of varnish on the lute back's beautiful curve . . .

He wouldn't forget again. In the afternoon

intermission he would slip out to try the door into Water Lane.

When intermission came, it brought no chance for escape. The sky had turned a leaden gray and rain gusted against the windows, but even if it hadn't been raining, he couldn't have gone. Every time he looked toward a door, or down a passage, there was Garland. He was never looking James's way, but he was there. In the end James stopped gazing out at the rain and went to watch four of the older boys play a card game they called "primero." Two others were playing what they called "tables," which turned out to be backgammon. The main attraction, though, was at the back of the schoolroom. There the rushes on the floor were less trampled down, and two wrestling matches were in progress. Lookouts posted outside the doors of the outer rooms guarded against interruption, and instead of cheering on their favorites, the spectators kept their voices low and danced up and down or waved their arms or punched each other in delight. The wrestlers were surprisingly rough, careful only of each other's faces. Little Trussell explained to James that if the Master or Mr. Evans or Mr. Moult appeared, everyone had to be seated at the tables, playing games and looking unruffled and undamaged. When one boy's nose did begin to bleed, after the others had helped stop it with handkerchiefs and a flood of advice, the referee declared, "No more for you after this, Mottram. I will not risk a beating because you have a delicate nose."

James was passing a window that looked out onto Playhouse Yard when he spotted a familiar shadowy figure at the mouth of the passage down from Carter Lane. Jack Garland—if it was Garland—was talking with a tall, stooping man with a beaky nose almost as pointed as the beak of his hat. After a moment they appeared to shake hands, but something about the movement made James think *Money!* almost as surely as if he had heard the *chink* of coins. Then Mr. Moult appeared, coming from the south side of the yard. Garland ducked back out of sight. The moment Mr. Moult stepped up into the entry porch, Jack slid out of the passage, caught up, and fell into step behind him. Indoors, the lookouts passed along the *Moult on the*

Way! alarm and boys scrambled to their places. Mr. Moult was in the quiet, orderly classroom before he looked behind him, and by then Garland had slipped in and was at the book cupboard, turning the pages of a fat Latin volume. James was uneasy. He didn't trust Garland. What was he up to? And why was his purse never empty when the rest of the Children never had more than their piddling sixpence a week from the queen? He never joined in their card games, so he hadn't won the money. . . .

After supper that evening Mr. Moult sat at one end of the table with James, correcting him as he recited the forms of the fifth-declension noun *meridies* and the twenty-six tenses and two participles of the first-conjugation verb *amare*. Jack and Nell played at chess, and Mrs. Moult stitched a wool felt cap for small Alice.

James, even as he recited, kept the corner of his eye on Jack. Why had he come to Mugwell Street in the place of one of the other new boys? He was perfectly at ease, but the Moults seemed somehow—

self-conscious? Wary? Wary of a kid who was—what? Eleven? Twelve? How could that make sense? Unless—unless Jack was blackmailing Mr. Moult about moonlighting as a teacher for the school next door. What had he said? *"He thinks the Master and Mr. Evans don't know."* James shifted uncomfortably on his stool. He was probably imagining things.

"Parrett!" Mr. Moult called him back to the Latin verbs with a sharp smack of a wooden spoon across his knuckles.

"Yes, sir," James said, and tried to remember where he had left off.

fifteen

THURSDAY WAS FOR JAMES ANOTHER DAY OF lessons and rehearsal and another evening of being stuffed with Latin. He awoke late in the darkness of Friday morning to the voices of Mrs. Moult and the maidservant in the kitchen below. By the time he had pulled on his new Chapel clothes and hurried down, a coach was at the door.

After breakfast at Blackfriars, the day was all rehearsal at St. John's, with the official dress rehearsal before the Master of the Queen's Revels in the afternoon. James spent the morning until Act Five was called with Mr. Browne in a small room off the *Cynthia's Revels* rehearsal room, learning new songs— and finding out how little he knew about speaking well and clearly, standing, and even breathing. Afterward, when he was called in for his appearance as Thauma, he had to strap on the high "buskins"—a kind of elevator shoe—to move with a gliding step through the final scenes. It felt strange, but then it was supposed to *look* strange, so perhaps it was all right.

So, on the whole, was the dress rehearsal in the great chamber at St. John's Gate. Any part that Edmund Tilney, Master of the Revels, disapproved of would have to be changed, so his approval was an even greater relief to Benjamin Jonson than to the Master and Mr. Evans. At the end of the afternoon Jonson went off in search of a tavern to celebrate his genius. The Master and Mr. Evans went home to their families, and James and Jack Garland rode with the Children in one of their carriages to the Children's lodgings at Mrs. Matcham's for supper as a sort of celebration before they were taken on to Mugwell Street.

Mrs. Matcham provided an excellent supper of roast beef and roast mutton, with buttered turnips and winter cabbage, and apple tart and cheese. Afterward she showed James and Jack the addition that was to provide a study room and a new bedchamber above it. Both had fireplaces and good oak floors and ready-to-be-plastered walls. "'Twill be ready before the New Year," she said. "The plaster must cure dry before 'tis distempered, and that dry, too. 'Twould not do to lodge fine voices here while 'tis not yet cured of dampness."

Garland raised the makeshift canvas covering over the window space to look out into the tiny garden. Just below the window, snug up against the alley wall, a new shed leaned its back against the study-room-to-be. "Nice," he said.

James went to look, and saw that it was. *Nicely climbable*, he thought, with a flick of a look at Garland.

One of the coaches returned James and Jack to Mr. Moult's house, where they found the kitchen warm and steamy. A tub that looked like half of a very large barrel stood waiting in the middle of the floor. "The children all are abed," Mrs. Moult explained. "We bath tomorrow night, but you must be fresh for your play."

The hot bath left James feeling as if he were a puppet and someone had cut the strings. He dragged up the stairs in clean underlinen and a fresh shirt and climbed into the bed the maid had just warmed with a warming pan. A long, full day, and an odd numbness in his heart pitched him into so deep a sleep that he didn't even twitch when he dreamed that Jack had sat up in bed and crept down the stairs. *I'll look next time*, he promised himself vaguely.

Saturday rolled past James as if he were looking down on it from above. He was tired, he told himself, and except for Sundays, every day in this world—this time—was much like every other for the Children. A coach appeared at Mugwell Street before seven, and after morning prayers and writing out the Latin or French composition assigned the day before, came breakfast, Latin or French lessons, intermission and, for all but James, dancing lessons—today a rehearsal of the dances in the between-acts interludes. James, as usual, had lessons with Mr. Browne. The only difference on this Saturday was that during the morning, carts had brought from St. John's the great trunk loads of costumes for the evening's performance. After the noon meal the orchestra—

its mandolins, violins, viols, pandoras, lutes, flutes, and table organ played by sixteen of the Children who did not appear in the first three acts—ran through their hourlong before-the-play concert. Afterward each of the four song-and-dance interludes for between the acts rehearsed again, in costume. James, who was down in the little chamber with Mr. Browne, having his knuckles rapped for awkward fingering on the lute strings, missed seeing all but the last interlude. Even that brief taste amazed him. The boys might wrestle and play their own indoor version of football like bone-crunching demons when the masters were out of the classroom, but they sang and danced and played like angels. They might be driven to it by the Master's sharp tongue, heavy hand, and demand for perfection (and the frustrated roars and delighted praise of their poet), but James thought they were amazing—every baby, bully, good guy, and sneak of the lot.

In the late afternoon Mr. Browne came to sit beside James on a gallery bench to watch the Master drive the players in Act Three over a difficult passage at a new and faster pace. James heard his friendly chatter only dimly, nodding to his ". . . so our plays are considered by the Revels office to be but rehearsals for its presentation before the queen, yet the public pay handsomely to see them—twice the sixpence they pay to watch a play in the open air. The Globe and Fortune would be happy to fare so well."

He leaned closer. "Perhaps I am not meant to tell you, Parrett," he murmured, "but why not? The Master tells me that he has listened outside the door another time or two to our lessons, and he is pleased. He says that in perhaps a week your song may be added to the interludes."

That did sink in. James felt . . . he didn't know what he felt. He had discovered that he loved to sing, but he did not know how he would feel if he had to—*when* he had to—stand up in front of an audience to do it. In every other thing he had done, he had been a watcher and listener. There had been times when he envied Reenie, who was a reacher-out, a heart-toucher, but he always told himself that either you were made that way or you weren't. Reenie was. He wasn't.

Reenie . . . Why was he thinking of her now as Reenie

and not Mama, as if she was just this singer he loved to listen to?

As the thought of her washed over him, he found it hard to breathe. The brilliance of the theatre and the spectacle on its stage dimmed, and the desperation that had faded into detachment flooded back. This past was a net to trap not only him, but his heart. . . .

Coming from supper nearby at Mrs. Matcham's, James saw coaches already crowded to a standstill in Carter Lane, and backed up as far as St. Paul's Cathedral in Creed Lane, Ludgate, and St. Peter's Hill. Later, from a window in the tiring room he looked down onto an unreal throng. Gold and silver lace glinted, jewels flashed, plumes waved, and white ruffs gleamed in the glare of the torches around Playhouse Yard. One young man with a pointed beard and a great pearl earring wore a pleated ruff James was sure was as wide as a manhole cover. He couldn't turn his head, so had to turn his whole body in order to see each new person to whom he spoke. Some others were frilled, furbished, and painted almost as fantastically as the featherbrained courtiers in Mr. Jonson's play. Once during a rehearsal James had heard Mr. Jonson shout out, "*Wit,* my boy, not clowning! The play is *serious.* We are teaching the foolish to be wise!" James had thought it only more of the poet's high-flown opinion of himself, but it seemed that his targets were real.

James had no chance to see the audience close at hand as they bought and snacked on apples and nuts and listened to the concert of popular songs and dance music. The music, laughter, and applause that reached the boys waiting on benches in the tiring room was muffled by the wall between it and the stage, and the doors at top and bottom of the backstage stairs. James's curiosity had to wait until Thauma's appearance in Act Five. When he and Phronesis and Time at last made their stately, gliding entrance, he had a dizzy moment. Chandeliers glimmered with candles. Footlight lamps glowed in seashell sconces. Both audience and players glittered in their finery. All that James, gliding ten inches off the floor in his buskins, could think was, *This isn't real. None of it is real.*

For them it was. Not for him. He mustn't let

it be. But he was frightened that already the future where he belonged was slipping away. . . .

After the audience was gone, the chandeliers were lowered and their candles and the others snuffed out, and Mr. Evans disappeared with the admissions boxes to count the evening's take. Benjamin Jonson wound down from his fury at the man who had shouted out, "Long-winded jackasses!" and the seven showily dressed ladies and gentlemen who stalked out without waiting for the interval. And last of all, after the traffic jam had unraveled, a coach returned James and Jack to Mugwell Street. James was so numb from the strangeness and the long day that he felt as if he were still wearing the buskins as he stumbled up the Moults' stairs.

As he stripped off his jacket and doublet and trunk hose by the fire, all he could think was, *You have to wake up the next time Garland gets up in the night. You have to. If you stay here, you'll be someone else. You won't be you.*

In spite of all of James's promises to himself, all of his warnings, Latin, dancing lessons, lute lessons,

Christmas, and the second Saturday-evening perform-ance of *Cynthia's Revels* came and went. If Garland had taken any more late-night jaunts, James had slept too deeply to waken. Nighttime or day, Jack remained a puzzle. On Monday morning, the classroom buzzed excitedly over a rumor of the return to London of some nobleman or other, a name and bit of news that meant nothing to James. It must have meant something to Jack Garland, though, because he went the queasy shade of white-skin paleness Gran called "green." He shut up, too, so that one morning passed without his whispered mockery or sharp-edged imitations of the masters or servants.

As for Christmas, which James and Jack spent with the rest of the Children at Mrs. Matcham's, the day seemed all prayers and church services and meals except for the half hour when the boys divided into two parts to wage a war of carols. The house rang with "Make We Merry" pitted against "Noël, noël, noël, noël," and *"Verbum caro factum est!"* against "Now We Sing with Angels." Timid Mr. Matcham quite enjoyed it, but the din so rattled Mrs. Matcham that in the end she forced a truce by bringing out the half of the great Christmas cake that she had kept back for their supper.

Neither the din nor the cake mattered much to James. He went where he was told, did what he was told, sang what he was told. Fear that he was losing himself had seeped into his bones, and turning off seemed to make it easier to keep a part of his old self alive, easier to keep repeating to himself that this was all wrong, that he didn't belong. That if he let go, he would be swallowed up.

sixteen

JAMES AND JACK WERE RETURNED TO THE HOUSE on Mugwell Street well after supper. The Moults, parents and children, were in bed. The old manservant opened the door to the boys, locked it after them, and then took himself off to the shed in the garden and his own bed with a look that made James think the Moults might be glad to be rid of their guests, however well the Master might be paying them for the room. The young Moults would have their bedroom back, and the servants their garret.

Later, an hour or more after he had pulled the covers up to his chin, the sound of creaking wood somewhere outside awakened James, and he sat up. A sleepy-eyed look out of the little garret window beside his bed into the moon-pale garden showed him Jack clambering over the paling fence from a ladder propped against it. James pushed the blankets back and swung his feet to the floor. Because he had been so cold from the first night on, he had begun to change into the brown suit for going to bed, so that all he had to do now was snatch up his shoes and pull the old cloak from atop the covers. Two blankets might be enough for Garland, but for someone used to central heating in winter, they were about as warm as two sheets. Even with the cloak on top he had still been so cold that being up and moving felt far better than curled up and quivering. On the way down the stairs to the kitchen he tried to move quietly, but almost every tread gave a faint squeak. A bed creaked in the front bedroom, but no one called out.

Because Garland had a head start, James felt his way into the front parlor instead of out to the kitchen door into the garden. In the parlor he pulled on his shoes. Luckily the key was in the lock. He unlocked the front door, slipped out, relocked it, and with the key in his pocket, stepped into the street.

The moon was up, but barely over the rooftops.

He saw no sign of Garland back down Mugwell Street, but off in the other direction, where the street turned at a right angle to run parallel to the old City Wall, a small figure trotted down the middle of the road. James followed. On his right the street was lined with houses, but on his left there was only the fenced-off strip of an empty building lot and the City wall with St. Giles's church tower peering over it, until he came to a high, turreted gateway in the City wall. By then Jack Garland had vanished.

The great gate and the roadway that passed over the City ditch were closed for the night, but the postern door beside the gate stood open for late travelers, and the gateman dozed on his bench inside the passageway. Taking a chance, James slipped past and through the postern passage over the ditch, once a moat filled with water, that ran along the wall. Beyond, the way divided to the left and right past a large, roofed conduit fountain. Water splashed loudly in the stillness. Up the narrow way to the left, a small figure flitted through the moonlight between the house shadows, then turned out of sight.

James followed.

Around the far corner, James saw Jack stop outside a tall, square silhouette of a building with a turreted tower at the middle of the front. He tried one door, and then moved to the second, which was locked as well. After a moment he set off again. James, when he reached the high, square building, could see from close-to that its corner posts and doorway—and probably much more—were richly carved, and that its hanging sign showed a great wheel. He could not make out the carved letters below the wheel, but along the top of a framed notice board beside the doorway was carved the name *The Fortune*. The Fortune on Beech Street. Mr. Browne had said that Jack Garland's brother Tom was a player at the Fortune.

James almost had to press his nose against the paper pinned on the board to read what was printed there.

This Weeke

—A Play—

Fortune's Tennis

Halfway down the list of players' names was 𝔗𝔥𝔬𝔪𝔞𝔰 𝔊𝔞𝔯𝔩𝔞𝔫𝔡. Was Jack only visiting his brother, then?

Jack himself was already past the stone cross in the middle of the next street crossing. A few yards past Golden Lane, as the cross street was named on the side of the corner house, a white horse on a hanging sign gleamed in the light of a lantern. There Jack vanished again. James, reaching the sign, peered into the passage and saw a long courtyard and lamps along an upper gallery, and heard laughter and singing. A boy was leading a horse back through the yard and into a second passage. James was about to step inside, but drew back when he caught sight of Jack peering in at the door of what, at a guess, was a bar—a "drinking room." The laughter, the rowdy snatches of song, and a figure that stumbled out and up the stairs to one of the gallery chambers made that much clear.

Young Garland stayed in the shadows by the drinking-room door for what might have been ten or fifteen minutes. Then, as a group of men crowded out, he retreated farther back along the inner yard.

James backtracked along the front of the inn as far as

the corner and watched as the men came out onto the street, turned to the right, and strode on without another word among them. Jack's head popped out of the entryway, and when the men were well away, he followed.

He was up to something, but what? Baffled, James hurried after them. He was drawn as much by curiosity as by the hope that their westward path would take him across some street he knew. At the next crossing the men went straight on. After a few yards, the lamplit house fronts lining the narrowed street began to seem familiar to James, and before long he recognized Long Lane, where he had first encountered Jack, and from his hurried passage along it with Plumed Hat, for he still thought of Jack's brother by that name. When the odd little procession reached Smithfield, it turned down to the left, along the side of the field across and away from the City bars at Cowcross Street and the way to the Clerk's Well beyond.

James's curiosity about what Jack was up to faded against the pull of the stairway down to the Well. He turned away toward the bars.

• • •

At Clerkenwell Green, St. James's church was locked fast. He had known it would be, and he tugged at the iron-ring handle with no hope, but found it hard to let go. Hopelessly, he pushed at the great gate to the Close. Down the slope of the road and around the corner he climbed up onto the corner of the well pool to push at the door there, but it was barred. Climbing down, he followed the wall north along the old garden to its end, stubbornly, angrily, tearfully, and turned into the field to follow it on. Somewhere the wall had to be broken down. Somewhere an apple tree must hang over it. Somewhere workers in the old, hedged field would surely have left a fallen tree, a long-forgotten ladder. Somewhere . . .

The wall was whole on the north and then the east, and all the way south again to its end at a fence that ran along Clerkenwell Road. The sliver of a moon watched as James stumbled into the church porch to sit, arms around his knees, leaning his forehead against the door.

It was half an hour or more before he lifted his head. *Garland.*

He had to be back before Jack Garland was. . . .

• • •

On the following night Jack was up and gone before James could swing his unwilling legs to the floor. He fumbled into his shoes, caught up his cloak, and crept downstairs. In the parlor he found the front-door key still in the lock, so he knew Jack had gone out the back and over the fence again. James locked the door behind him and hurried off toward Cripplegate in hope that Jack had gone the same way as before. By the time he stepped out into the road at the far end of the postern-gate passage and turned up Whitecross Street, his eyes had sharpened in the starlight. In a moment he spied a movement as Jack's shadowy shape, far ahead, turned into the street that ran past the Fortune Theatre and the White Horse Inn. When James himself reached the Fortune, he saw dim lamplight in a window and at the entry. If Jack hadn't gone on to the White Horse to lie in wait for and follow the men he had so mysteriously followed before, he must be inside, with his brother.

The light in the window winked out before Jack showed himself. Shadows moved in the entryway. One man paused under the lantern to murmur a word or two to the fellow behind him, and James was startled to recognize a hat and face. The second man was Plumed Hat—Jack's brother.

Tom Garland reached up to unhook the lantern, and the shadows moved out into the street. As they hurried off in the same direction as before, James counted five. They were well ahead before Jack slipped out of a dark doorway across the road to follow the bobbing lantern, and James was baffled once again. Jack's own brother, and he shadowed him like a detective, or spy? But *why* would Jack be lying in wait for his own brother?

Trailing behind the men and their nimble shadows, James puzzled over the strangeness of it. In their wake he picked his way across Aldersgate Street and along Long Lane, and at Smithfield wavered for a long uncertain moment. The men veered off to the left past St. Bartholomew's Hospital on the same path that they had traveled before, with Jack darting behind from one dark shadow to the next. James, without at all having decided to, found himself running past the hospital and along the edge of West Smithfield, past dimly lit inns and still noisy taverns, down into a street of shops he had never seen before.

On the way back. I'll go to Clerkenwell Close on the way back, he promised himself.

He lost sight of the men, but still caught glimpses of the flitting shadow that was Jack Garland. He tried to fix streets and landmarks in his mind as he went: three lanes that came together, a public water-conduit house where water from the conduit pipe splashed like a fountain into its cistern, and a little farther ahead a stone bridge. From the bridge he had a clear view ahead and, thanks to their bobbing lantern, spotted the five men on up the hill as they took the first downward turning on the left. He could not see Jack, but knew he would be close on their heels.

The turning was a narrow lane, and dark, and James, following, was forced at times to feel his way along the housefronts. At the bottom he came out onto a wider street lined with shops and houses. Late as it was, a few coaches and riders still rumbled and trotted past, and James, wary of arousing curiosity, kept to the darker, northern side of the way. Half a mile or so farther on, where the houses began to be much larger and the road ran through a roofed-over gateway with bars like those at Cowcross Street, and in the center a crossbar gate, he lost sight of both the players and Jack.

What he saw were little knots of late passersby lingering in front of the next great house on the left and staring. Five or six coaches were lined up along the side of the street, and servants and ragged young boys acted as hitching posts for the dozen or more waiting horses. One of the boys was Jack Garland. *Clever little sneak*, James thought. Clever Jack, with a horse to hide behind, was working his way toward the gateway for a better view of the house.

From the shelter of a doorway across the street, James stared up at the great house with its guards and gated passage and all its windows lavishly lit by chandeliers bright with scores of candles. From time to time, as men entered or came out, the guards still stood stiffly in place and seemed not to notice. *Almost as if they're there for decoration*, James thought. What would a player like Tom Garland have to do with a place like this?

It was half an hour or more before Tom Garland and his four friends came out. Jack retreated quickly, handing off his horse to a shoeless boy who wore a ragged blanket for a cloak. By the time the startled boy could grin his thanks, Jack was already gone. The unsuspecting players, with their two young shadows, went back the way they had come, and at the White Horse Inn parted to go their separate ways. When they were safely gone, Jack went off at a run toward Cripplegate, with James hurrying behind. James was careful to keep close, but not too close. At the postern gate the guard drowsed on his bench and both boys slipped through without waking him.

James barely made it through the front door, up the stairs, out of his shoes, and under the bedcovers before Jack could come over the fence and in and up.

He was almost asleep before he remembered the Clerk's Well. He had forgotten. He had the chance to go, had been on his way, and had forgotten.

seventeen

IN THE WEEK THAT FOLLOWED, THE DAYS BLURRED one into the other. Almost every one of those days, Jack Garland went missing during intermission, but no one pointed out his absence to the Master or any other of the adults. He returned each time more sour than he had left, and James each time had felt curiosity pluck hard at his sleeve, but he had no chance to follow or to slip away to the Clerk's Well. His intermissions, by the Master's order, were spent in learning the songs and church music the other Children knew, as well as rehearsing "Fair Cynthia." He felt like a ball snapped from one pair of hands to another in an endless round. Practicing. Rehearsing. Fittings. Learning how to unfold himself majestically out of the trap door while the platform was cranked upward from the cramped space under the stage. Practicing walking in the high-soled buskins—while wearing a mask with eyes almost impossible to see through. Rehearsing again.

He was to sing "Fair Cynthia" on Saturday at the end of the last interlude, with two others of the Children to join in the chorus. Even more amazing was the news that he was to sing it dressed as "A Night Bird" in a robe of layers of black taffeta cut to resemble shiny feathers, and a beaked bird mask that was as eerie as it was beautiful. He felt numb, and as unreal as he looked in this new costume.

To make everything more uncomfortable, the more attention the Master, Mr. Browne, and the other men paid him, the more they smiled and whispered in corners, the cooler the boys grew. Once it was clear their masters meant to give him some special part to cap the final interlude, the coolness grew chillier. The eight who, like himself, were snatched away from their own lives had been snatched to be actors, and all they envied James for was the attention. The singers, though, began to resent and ignore him, for those who had sung in the

Chapel for years felt so fine a chance should have gone to one of them, and never to a foreigner.

Late every night James returned to Clerkenwell, but not by Garland's route to Long Lane. By keeping his eyes open, he had discovered that he could avoid the Fortune Theatre, the inn, and Jack by turning past the church of St. Giles Cripplegate, and up Redcross Street instead of Whitecross. A few yards before Redcross Street reached the crossroad past the White Horse Inn, a long alleyway branched off to the left and brought him out onto Beech Street well past the inn. From there he trusted to caution and luck to keep from being spotted.

His luck never went further than that.

At Clerkenwell Close the church door was always locked, the great gates always too stout, the well door always barred, and the walls all around too high to climb. Three nights in a row he sat for a while with his back against the door above the well pool, the door that led to the stairs, *his* stairs. Afterward he made his way back to Mugwell Street. Each time his weariness deepened, the way grew longer, and the way back longer still.

On the Thursday night James returned from the Clerk's Well stumbling with lack of sleep. When he passed the White Horse only one window still showed a light, and the Fortune was dark. He saw no sign of Jack, and reached the postern door at Cripplegate just as the late-night gateman was stirring himself to close it.

James tried to hurry, but could not. The gateman saw him and waited.

Once through, he had only a short distance along London Wall to go to reach the top of Mugwell Street. He almost turned an ankle in a muddy rut, and as he fumbled in the pocket at his waist for the key he peered down to watch his footing. The hand that shot out of the shadows by the fence along the vacant ground caught him off balance and swung him hard against the palings.

"Black Canary? Black Parrot, more like!" Jack Garland hissed. "Why do you follow me? Who has set you to follow me?"

For a moment James's mind was too blank with

surprise for an answer. Then he pulled free and pushed himself upright. He was too tired to watch his tongue. "No one, you little sneak! Who would care? I was curious, that's all. Wouldn't you be if *I* went out the back door and over the fence?"

"You saw me from the window, then?" Moonlight glittered in Garland's eyes, and then they narrowed. "Why did you follow?"

"Wouldn't you?" James rubbed his shoulder. "I was curious. I'm sorry, okay? Can we go in now? I'm cold."

Jack kept hold of his cloak. "Once is curiosity. Twice is spying. Three times and more is—what is three times, Parrett?"

"All right!" James held up his hands. "I wondered why you'd be following your own brother. Or why you've been going around looking like your best friend just died. I thought I might find out. But you're right. It's none of my business. I won't follow you again."

"You are mocking me. I have no friend but my brother." Jack peered at him in distrust. "But take care. You have secrets, too. Keep clear of me, or I'll lift the cover off *your* stewpot to have a sniff."

James stiffened and stepped away. "And what stewpot is that?"

Instead of answering, Garland slipped past him and in a moment had vanished into the alley alongside the Moults' house. James stood rooted in the middle of the street as alarm slid its cold fingernail down his spine. *Garland had followed him to the Clerk's Well.*

But when? Tonight? What had he seen?

A window creaked open nearby, and a raspy voice called out, "Who's there in the street? Get along, or I'll loose the dog on thee!"

James shook himself and stumbled on.

The key turned easily enough in the lock on the front door, but the lock bolt snapped back with a loud *snock!* James froze, waiting for the creak of floorboards above. When none came, he slipped in, relocked the door, and crept up the stairs to his bed. Jack was just taking off his shoes. Neither boy looked at the other as they climbed into bed and pulled the bedcovers over them.

On Friday, the day after New Year's, when the coach came to Mugwell Street to collect Mr. Moult and the boys, a cart came with it to collect the three beds and the boys' clothing. The new room at Mrs. Matcham's was painted and aired and waiting. James, when he saw the cart, dashed back to thank Mrs. Moult. He liked her and was sorry to go—and sorrier still because he was a little bit afraid of Mrs. Matcham. She was plump and jolly but had small sharp eyes that made you wonder what you had done wrong.

When he returned to the street, Jack was already in the coach, and scowling.

Not long after their arrival at Blackfriars, while the Children were finishing their breakfast, a Queen's Messenger came clattering into Playhouse Yard on horseback. Buswell was sent to investigate, and returned to the refectory to call the Master out. The boys were in the classroom when Master Giles returned with his mouth a thin, tight line. His eyes looked as if they would have shot sparks if they could have. His son-in-law, Robinson, looked up from the foot of the table.

"Master? What is't?"

The Master took a deep breath as he sat down again. "What is't? Why, nothing much. Only that the

Master of the Revels sends from Whitehall to say that Queen Elizabeth will not see our play on Twelfth Night day. We are to entertain her instead with music and dance alone." His voice was tight. "Four days' notice. What am I to do?"

The boys held still, flicking their eyes from one end of the table to the other like spectators at a tennis match.

Mr. Robinson grimaced. "Someone at Court has not liked seeing courtiers lectured from a stage. Who is to tell our poet?"

The Master forgot his irritation enough to give a little *hmph!* of laughter. "Not I. I shall send Gowthrop to Westminster to tell him. By the time Jonson walks here from Tothill Street, perhaps his temper will have cooled a little."

"And then?"

"I will tell him there is nothing to be done for his *Cynthia* for now, but that we will use the songs from the play in the queen's entertainment."

Master Giles sat for a long, frowning moment and pulled at his beard. "They and the songs and dances from our interludes will not make up much more than an hour. We will need to fill two. I shall send for Dr. Bull, and you will summon the dancing master."

He turned to Mr. Moult. "After your Latin lessons, sir, the boys are to have a long intermission. Those who wish may remain, to study under your eye. Mr. Robinson will escort the others to their lodging and they will return here at noon for their dinner. After the meal Mr. Browne will bring Parrett to me in the little chamber."

Around the table eyes gleamed, but no one risked a smile. James saw Jack Garland sitting bent over his Latin book with unusual attention, but as soon as the Master was gone, his head came up. James gave a little snort to himself and opened his own Latin book with a sigh. He didn't look up as Mr. Moult directed the boys who were going with Mr. Robinson to stand and line up in twos, and he was startled by a sharp tug at his sleeve from someone passing behind him. He looked up with a frown. Garland.

To James's surprise Jack Garland gave a little jerk of his head and motioned him to join the back of the line beside him. When James didn't move, he gave a hard stare and mouthed words that looked like "Come, or be sorry." James's curiosity gave him a nudge, and besides, he decided, if Jack Garland could be trusted for anything, it would be for following through on a threat. He closed his book and stood.

Jack said nothing until Mr. Robinson and the head of the line had turned the corner from the passage out of Playhouse Yard into Carter Lane. Then he signed to James to drop back so that Frost and Mottram, just ahead, could not overhear him.

"Say nothing. I will explain on our way. Once we are in the new room at Mistress Matcham's, shed your crimsons, don your old suit and jerkin and cloak, and follow me. For now, not a word." He stalked on, catching up again to Jack Frost and Mottram.

Everything went well at the house in Knightrider Street until, dressed in his own old street clothes, Jack turned to the window overlooking the shed roof. "The foul fiend curse it!" he hissed in sudden fury, "*It will not open!*"

James dropped his cloak and went to see. And it

did not. Instead of the usual casement that could be unfastened and swung outward, only a narrow transom at the top opened; the rest of the window was fixed in place. "What will we do?"

Jack looked at the older James with scorn. "Walk out the front door, you ninny. There's naught else to be done."

Nervous and—however mistrustful—impressed by Jack's cool nerve, James followed him down the house's spiral stair and out through the entryway. From the rowdy shouts and bumps in the new study room, it sounded as if all of the other boys were there. In the entry hall itself, a sullen maidservant putting down clean rushes saw them go out into the street, but showed no interest. Jack set off at a half run up St. Peter's hill toward the cathedral. James followed him up, then down Ludgate Hill and through the great gate, but stopped in the middle of Fleet Bridge to call after him, "Hi, where are we going? And why?"

All impatience, Jack came back only far enough so that he wouldn't have to shout. "To Essex House, to hear a sermon."

James stared. "A *sermon?* You're joking." Watching Garland's face, he saw a struggle among impatience, frustration, and fright—and anger at not easily having his own way. In the end, Jack came back to pull James along by his arm.

"My brother Tom . . . my brother has put his head into a lion's mouth, and I must pull it out," he said desperately. "Ever since my lord Essex returned to London in spite of the queen's black frowns, my brother Tom and many others of the players have fallen in love again with his fine looks and finer words. They listen to those who whisper that the queen must name the earl to take the crown when she dies. Such words are sedition, and can earn them their deaths, but the whisperers call the lords of her council wolves and jackals, and her a foolish old woman. They say that the Earl of Essex is her true servant, and that she has wronged him greatly by turning away from him."

"So?" James watched him warily. He had heard snatches of these things, but paid them no attention. They had nothing to do with him.

"'So? So *they* all are the fools." Jack's eyes were sus-
piciously close to tears. "I think some are so far gone in
foolishness that they begin to make plots. But old or no,
the queen is as sharp as a needle. Her spies are everywhere. They hear these whispers. They hear my lord
Essex tell the crowd that only he is their true friend. He
welcomes them to his house, and invites hotheaded
Puritan preachers to blow on the fire with their sermons. It will all end with the headsman and the hang-
man. But my brother only laughs when I tell him so."

James hurried along beside him. "Maybe he's
right," he said as they crossed over Fleet Bridge. "How
do you know he isn't?"

Jack threw him a bleak glance and looked away.
"Because I am a listener. I listen, and tell what I hear,
and I carry messages for two of the queen's agents who
cannot be seen together."

James stopped dead in surprise, then hurried along
Fleet Street to catch up. It explained so many odd
things that he believed it.

"Did you tell your brother *that?*"

"I would have. I tried, but he said I believed such

things only because I was in the queen's service, and protected from the real world. He grew angry, and I stopped, for I could not bear to have him hate me for a spy. So I have brought you. You must tell him for me."

James let out a half-breathless wheeze of laughter. "*I* must? You *are* crazy. How am I supposed to know what's true and what's not? I don't! Why would he believe me?"

Jack slid him a sideways glance. "You will hear what these preacher-folk and my lord Essex's friends say, and then you will believe me. Then you will tell my brother what your uncle, Stephen Parrot, has told you."

"What uncle?" James stared. "I don't have an uncle here. Not here or in—Africa," he added hastily. Still, the name Stephen Parrot did faintly ring a bell.

"Yes, you do." Jack turned a narrow, catlike look on him. "Think back. The morning when first you came to us? Poet Jonson asking how you spell your name?"

James frowned, remembering. "He asked because— it was something about how someone with the other spelling could stink up a room."

"Yes. Because Stephen Parrot is a spy, and the poet

hates spies. He was in prison once because of things said in a play he helped to write. They put spies in his cell to try to trap him into speaking against the government."

"And Parrot was one of them?"

"I think he must have been. But half of London whispers that Parrot is a spy. My brother will have heard of him."

James frowned. "Say that I talk to your brother. What am I supposed to tell him?"

Jack swallowed, as if the words were too full of fright for speaking. "That the queen is in a great rage at my lord's defiance. That he and his followers are on the edge of treason. And that treason's reward is a rope around the neck."

James took a deep breath. He knew that he would do it. Jack might be a rat, but he loved his brother. And James liked his brother. Owed him, in fact. After all, Tom Garland had rescued him from the river. Or was going to. Even so, caution made him stop and ask, "All right, I could say that. But I don't like you, so why should I?"

Jack's eyes narrowed. "Because I can get you into the old nunnery at Clerkenwell."

eighteen

FLEET STREET ENDED AT TEMPLE BAR, WHERE THE City of London ended and Westminster began. From that point on the street's name was The Strand, and James recognized Essex House, the first great house on the left, as the one he had watched from the doorway opposite on the night he followed Jack. It looked as rich by day, but smaller now that he could see the near-palace next beyond it.

The crowd at Essex House was much larger than it had been on the night James followed Jack there. Most who ventured through the gate were men, mostly young, some richly dressed, many who were not. Citizens and their wives, soldiers and students, watermen and porters, and boys in the blue cloaks of apprentices milled around in the large central courtyard. James caught a glimpse of Jack as he wriggled through the press of bodies.

Once in, he saw that a sort of podium or high railed platform had been set up in the center of the stone-paved yard, for a large crow of a man in black, a preacher. He stood there, well above the heads of the crowd, and prayed at the sky in a loud voice. He called down God's blessing on the Earl of Essex and his works, and His wrathful judgment upon the earl's enemies. James guessed that the tall, slender man, brown-haired and ginger-bearded, who stood listening with respectful attention on a balcony on the far side of the courtyard was the famous Earl of Essex. Several other richly dressed men stood with him.

Ignoring the curious stares, James followed as Jack snaked easily through the crowd in search of his brother, but however close behind Jack he kept, the way closed tight in front of him. He had to struggle to keep up. They found the five players from the Fortune standing up on the broad rim of a fountain in a corner of the courtyard.

One of the players caught sight of Jack and beckoned. "Come up, Jack, lad," he called in a carrying whisper. "You can see but little from down there."

Jack shook his head. "I cannot. Tom, will you come out? I must speak with you. Please come."

Tom Garland frowned. "*Now*, Jack? Not now! Why, great things are a-brew here. Would you have me miss the sight of 'em?" Seeing James wriggling closer, he cocked his head at Jack. "Is that the lad you call your Master's parrot? Why are the two of you here and not at your lessons?"

A convincing tear glistened down Jack's cheek. "'Tis trouble, Tom. Real trouble."

Tom gave his young brother a searching look, half doubtful, half worried, and then with a sigh stepped down from his perch and followed the two boys out through the crowd to the street.

In a tavern not far back along Fleet Street from Essex House, Tom Garland settled them in a corner near the fire and made a sign to a potboy passing with two pitchers in each fist.

"Now, Jack! What 'real' trouble is this you have fallen into? Fleecing your fellow songbirds at cards? Selling Blackfriars Theatre candles to Dirty Nick in the Shambles?"

"No! I promised, didn't I?" Jack pleaded. "'Tisn't what I have done. 'Tis what James has told me. He overheard it from his uncle, Stephen Parrot."

Startled, Tom blinked at the name and turned a wary look on James. "What is it you have heard?" he asked slowly.

James took a deep breath and plunged in. "That the queen has her agents in the crowd at Essex House, watching who's there, and listening. Anybody who speaks against the council and the queen can be arrested for se-se—"

"Sedition." Tom Garland had gone pale.

"I heard that all they're waiting for is for the Earl to say something that's treason. But you and your friends? You've been followed every night since the Earl came back to London. And some days."

Jack had done the flat-out lying. James had told lies with the truth. He *had* heard about the queen's spies. From Jack. And Jack and he *had* followed Tom. James felt uneasy at the deception, but then Tom nodded and stood. "I must warn my friends of this," he muttered. "We are too easy recognized." He dropped the coins to pay for their ale on the table and hurried out as the potboy arrived with the three beakers.

James, once Tom was gone, took a long breath and then a swallow of ale. "All right. *How* are you going to get me into Clerkenwell Close after the gates are shut?"

"I don't know yet," Jack answered calmly. "I must discover first whether Tom truly believed you. And why you want to go there," he added calmly. He drained his beaker, rose, and wrapped his cloak around him. "Come, or we will be too late to change into our crimsons before our dinner."

James was almost more furious with himself than with Jack. He would have kicked the table leg, but it looked much more solid than his shoe. He jumped up instead and hurried after the slippery little weasel.

After the noon meal Master Giles paced up and down in the little chamber beside the kitchen. "Mr. Browne says that you are more than ready, Parrett. I have heard you sing my "Fair Cynthia" some dozen times, and I agree. On Twelfth Night day, you shall sing it to close our entertainment for the queen. For that we must furbish it up to make it a more splendid finish than tomorrow night's. I have decided that we shall have three trebles and three altos instead of one of each to sing the chorus, and they, not you, shall be dressed as night birds. You shall be Night herself, in blue-black velvet besprinkled with silver stars. On your head we shall have a silver crown of stars with black plumes." He waved his hands to sketch plumes. "The tailors and property-makers are already at work. The dancers who come before will divide, the night birds fly in, and Night rise up through the trap door on a dark cloud. *That* will bring them to their feet!"

James blinked, for a moment startled awake. Awake? More like dreaming with his eyes open. What could be more unreal than James Hackaday Parrett rising through a stage floor in star-spangled black velvet? More than anything he wanted to laugh, but he was afraid to. Mr. Browne's eyes crinkled a little as he watched James, but he didn't crack a smile. The Master was completely serious.

"This afternoon you will go to St. John's to be fit-ted. Later today and tomorrow we will rehearse the song yet again. Rumor is already abroad about our masked Night Bird. After Twelfth Day the town shall clamor to hear our Black Canary!"

"'Black Canary'?" Mr. Browne nodded a little doubtfully. "A name to catch the fancy. But, Master, why if you wish Parrett to be known as an African is he to wear a mask tomorrow?"

Master Giles smiled thinly. "Why *but* to catch the fancy? After all, our Parrett will be the queen's own Black Canary. What better than a surprise at Court to catch the curious, to set tongues a-wag, and to make our benches here to overflow."

James felt a flicker of resentment at the way the Master spoke of him as if he were a lute or viol on legs, but he was more bothered by the stir of excite-ment he felt in his middle. He took a deep breath and tried to smother it. The thought of singing before a queen, amazing or not, was part of a world he wanted to hold at arm's length. Needed to. *Had* to.

"Go, now," the Master was saying. "I must turn my mind to this pesky entertainment. Get you to St. John's." Still stroking his beard, he left the little chamber talking to himself.

"Poor Parrett," Mr. Browne said. "Why are you not pleased? Are you unwell?"

"No, sir. Only tired."

"You have not slept well at Moult's? You will be more at ease at Mrs. Matcham's, I think."

James winced. "Yes, sir," he said. But he knew that in a house with twenty-two boys, the Matchams and their servants, and a window that would not open, he was trapped.

Only the music was real.

On Saturday in the rehearsals, and even onstage during that night's performance, neither his fantastic getup nor the amazing, glittering audience could touch him while he sang. After the last interlude the tiring-room servants whisked his Night Bird gown and beaked mask away and brought Thauma's for Act

Five. A worried Mr. Browne fussed over him, steered him to the stage on cue, and when it was over saw him safely dressed in his crimson and delivered to Knightrider Street and Mrs. Matcham.

A canary in a cage, with only Jack Garland to help look for a key.

Or not.

nineteen

THOUGH THREE OTHER BOYS WERE SLEEPING IN
the same room, and one of them snoring loudly, Sunday
night was the first time since Friday that James had time
to debate with himself about what he should tell Jack.
Could tell. *Not one syllable too much,* he told himself,
and every syllable had to be true. He was always uncomfortable when he tried to lie, and though Tom Garland
seemed not to notice it, Jack was another matter. After
half an hour's tossing and squirming under the blankets,
James lay flat on his back to rehearse the best answer
he could come up with. *I want to see my father. My
mother's away, but my father looks after one of the houses in
the Close for the owner. I was staying with him. But the
gateman says I'm not allowed to be there. I used to sneak in*

through the church after the gate was shut, but the church is
locked at six o'clock. And now I can never get there in time.

"Oh," Jack said when he heard this on Monday morning on the walk to Blackfriars. He was clearly disappointed. Perhaps he had hoped for something more dramatic.

Or more profitable, James thought, suddenly alarmed. He knew enough to be wary of Jack even during morning prayers if ever he wore the "Hmm, let's see . . ." look he wore as they followed the end of the double line of Children into Playhouse Yard. He might be thinking of a way to "borrow" the church key to have a copy made for James, or where there might be a ladder to steal so that James could go over the wall at night. But what if he was thinking of vanishing *with* James in the direction of the Clerkenwell church some late afternoon? He might want to prowl through the old buildings or the new construction in search of something worth stealing. Or he might be suspicious about the part of the story in which a man who was supposed to be a music teacher was now a caretaker. He might even think

James's father was in hiding from enemies or the authorities, and be wondering how he could turn that knowledge into money. What if he went to spy him out, and saw the stair down to the well? The water carrier and the workmen may not have seen the hole in the air, but that didn't mean no one *could*. Perhaps it took an eager eye. Perhaps it took a child. . . .

"My father lost his job teaching the lute," James said in desperation. The lie jumped out almost before he had thought of it, and the flicker in Jack's eye told him that it hit the right target. "And we lost the lodgings that went with it," James added quickly. "My mother had to go away to work as—a baby nurse, and he became a watchman so we would have somewhere to sleep. My mother was supposed to return to London over a week ago, and then we were going to go back to America." At least he had managed to finish up with the truth—or something like it.

Jack nodded. "Later," he said as they entered the classroom.

At the start of morning intermission Jack was suddenly at James's side. "Stay here," he ordered.

When the room had emptied, he went to the classroom door and closed it. "No," he said as he came back. "I have no plan. I know a man, though, who knows of such things as the copying of keys. I will try to find him. But for now, will you write down for me all the words to the Master's 'Fair Cynthia'? I remember the first stanza, but little of the rest."

James blinked. "Why? You called it 'feeble stuff.'"

"And so it is." Jack gave him a sly grin. "But 'tis the Master's, and if he hears me whistle or sing it in the yard or hallway, he cannot think it flattery. I like to feed him a little honey each week."

"Like helping Mr. Robinson and the servants snare Thomas Clifton—and me?" James asked bleakly.

"Well . . . yes." Jack shrugged his shoulders and raised his eyebrows as if to ask, "What can I say?"

James sighed and began to write.

After the noon meal the Children of the Chapel Royal were taken to Paul's Wharf, where hired watermen rowed them in two boatloads upriver to Whitehall Palace Stairs. The river was at high tide, so they were able to step directly onto the stairs that led up to the palace Water Gate. At the top, guards opened iron-studded doors into a long, paved passage between buildings, for the palace was not one single building but dozens, grouped around great courts and gardens. Trussell, walking beside James in the line, pointed out the Chapel Royal and Great Hall on the left and kitchens and pantries to the right. The third pair of doors they passed through led out into the open and a great paved court surrounded on three sides by buildings. Straight ahead lay the main palace gate, but halfway there the line of boys were led aside through a short passage into another large courtyard, up a broad path, and onto a wide terrace.

The building that faced the terrace was a fantasy. It was more than a hundred feet long and a good forty feet high—not counting the roof above, which was supported on huge masts that once had been towering trees. The walls between the pillars looked like smooth gray stone, but as the boys drew near Bassocke exclaimed, "'Tis plaster! 'Tisn't stone at all!"

Henry Early, one of the boys who sang the services

in the palace's Chapel Royal, grinned. "Nor plaster. 'Twas built twenty years ago, they say, but here still it is, made of canvas and paint to fool the eye."

"But with osier or lath and plaster underneath, I warrant," said the practical Gedge, whose father was a builder.

The others gaped upward. Few of the boys except the Chapel singers had seen the great hall before, and not all of those had seen it from so close-to. A row of windows with diamond-shaped panes ran the length of the building just below the roofline and added to the magical effect, gleaming like pale gold in the wintry afternoon sunshine.

"What *is* it?" James asked in awe.

"The Banqueting House," answered Mr. Browne, who had come with the boys from Blackfriars. "It is the hall for the queen's great entertainments. The hammering you hear is the carpenters who hurry to finish the new stage for Twelfth Night tomorrow." He held open one leaf of the great double doors for them.

Inside, the boys stood crowded by the door, too amazed to stir. The great hall was all one huge unbelievable room, with the stage at one end, the royal dais and the queen's chair at the other, and ten narrow terraces for spectators that climbed up along the sides. The walls were richly decorated, painted all around with tall holly trees and trellises woven with painted ivy. The canvas-lined ceiling between the roof beams was colored like the sky, bright with clouds and golden sun and sunbeams at the stage end. That sky darkened to star-spangled night at the far end with the moon, the symbol of the goddess Diana—whose other name was Cynthia—and of Queen Elizabeth, above her chair. The queen's emblems of lion and unicorn, harp and thistle, all rich with gold, blazed at the four corners. Fantastic pendants made of wicker and decked with holly and ivy, or herbs and bright flowers spangled with gold, or colorful fruits spangled with gold—oranges, pomegranates, little pumpkins, grapes, and more—hung from the roof beams and trusses. The whole vast space seemed spangled with gold, and tall golden candelabra stood ready along the wide central aisle. Everywhere chandeliers were lowered so that workers could fill them with candles. At night it would be magical.

The boys had been brought to see the stage, to mark out their places and pace through their movements. The new stage, like their own, was four and a half feet above the floor, but the doorways and the stage house's inner stage were a little different. The Master directed the boys through all their movements for the songs and dances, but without the music.

The lift below the trap door through which James, as the starry Night, would rise was still unfinished, but as he stood on the stage, looking down the long hall toward the queen's chair, he was dazzled. For the past three weeks, whatever the Master and his people may have thought, James had been singing only to himself. For himself. Glad enough to please them, but too lost in this new-found world to care much. But perhaps . . . perhaps singing was not just the singer and the song. What, after all, was a song that no one heard? He stared down the long hall at the golden chair and wondered what it would be like to hold a great hall filled with people, and all glitter and shadows, spellbound. . . .

He knew he could do it. On Saturday night, with no real heart for it, he had brought it within reach.

He had caught and held a rustling, talkative between-acts audience. To go beyond that—to touch and enchant—might take only the *reaching*. With a great queen on a golden chair, and a crowd of hundreds in this amazing place, how could he not? The thought took his breath away.

Is this how Reenie feels?

The high windows had gone dark with the late winter afternoon before the Children finished the walk-through on the stage and were lined up to return to the river stairs and the boats. The bells of St. Martin's-in-the-Fields tolled the hour of four o'clock.

Jack Garland moved forward to slip in at the middle of the line for a change, and so was last to board the first boat. James, still caught in the excitement of the afternoon, had not seen this maneuver and didn't notice who it was who sat down on his right. Riding half in a dream downriver in the darkness past the great houses with their lamplit windows, he was startled awake as Jack knuckled him on the arm. "Wait for the end of the line when we reach the wharf," Jack whispered.

James stared at him blankly. "What?" he asked.

"We must wait for the end of the line," Jack breathed. "When the rest of us turn into Knightrider Street, you must keep on to St. Paul's and down Ludgate. Turn your cloak buff side out. The moon is near full tonight, but will not come out 'til late, so take care. I'll see that you are not missed 'til supper."

James stared at him in fright. "*Now?* Why now?"

"*Quiet!* Now, because it is not yet five o'clock. Because your church at the Clerk's Well still will be open. Because every other day we are at work or at lessons until six o'clock, and I have had no chance to steal the key or have another made." He shrugged. "But you must do as you please. I thought 'twas a matter of importance."

A matter of importance?

Nothing else mattered, James wanted to protest. But even as the thought spoke itself in his mind, he knew it was partly a lie. Singing mattered. From the simplest catch to the Master's uninspired "Fair Cynthia" to Mr. Jonson's "Queen and Huntress" or

Mr. Byrd's setting of the *Gloria*: All were pure pleasure in the singing. From stiff resistance, in three weeks he had come to that. Like the birds in the dawn chorus, he had come to shouting his heart up into the sky to burst in a red and silver shower.

And that was another lie.

Well, another half-truth. He could go home and sing. But not by candle and lamplight in a palace hall out of a fairy tale, before a great queen. She was an old lady, they said, but he wanted to *see* her. Like hobbit Sam Gamgee wanted to see the Elephaunt.

That was a lie too.

He wanted to take the Master's very ordinary song and turn it into magic, to enchant her. . . .

To make himself into Someone.

Whichever world he was in, he had held himself apart. Wanted to be James Himself, whoever that was, not Reenie's son, Phil's son, Grandma's grandson, the Master's Black Canary. He never asked or told anyone—anything much. Here the Children, in the end turned off by his starveling answers to questions about America or Africa or his parents, had stopped asking questions long before they turned cool to him.

Here some part, some corner of him, was always going to be a stranger.

The same might turn out still to be true at home, but there he would have choices. Here there were few of those. And face it: Here he would always be a Curiosity. . . .

And what if this were the right time and he missed it— and never found another? The thought pierced him like a shard of ice, and he shuddered.

"Well?" Jack hissed as the oarsmen shipped their oars and the barge slid into place alongside Paul's Wharf.

"I'll go," James said.

twenty

"ONE THING BEFORE I DO—" JAMES ADDED UNDER his breath as the line of boys formed on the wharf. "The day I got caught, why did you say, 'I heard him sing, but I was where I shouldn't have been, so Master Giles can't know the where and when.'"

Jack grinned his dangerous grin. "Last summer I was out all night one night at Kilburn, where our uncle lives. I was coming back across the fields to Clerkenwell Road when I saw a boy do cartwheels up the way by the well. A blackamoor. I was curious. Who would not be? So I followed you. I heard you sing. I had to watch for a good six months before I caught sight of you again."

Getting away was as easy as Jack said it would be, and as hard. James stopped for a moment in the doorway of the Paul's Head tavern to turn his cloak lining-side out. He remembered with a pang the warmth of the Paul's Head's fire on wet skin, his own confusion there, and Plumed Hat's kindness. *Shivering and dazed still,* he thought, and wished fiercely that he could have both worlds. He wished, too, that he could have thanked Tom Garland. But "For what?" Garland would have asked.

He pushed away from the orange-gold glow of the windows and cheerful din within and hurried on through the dusk. Past the shuttered bookshops in Paul's churchyard. Down Ludgate past St. Martin's Church. Out the City gate and north toward Smithfield. The farther he went, the more his steps lagged, and when at the top of Turnmill Street a breeze lifted as he came out where city street became country road at the foot of the Green, he wondered for a brief moment at the strange sharp, clean smell of it.

The going back was as easy as the getting away. Because that was so, it seemed to James the hardest thing he had ever done.

The church was open. The old gentleman and his small charges, struggling now through the *Book of Proverbs*, had no ears for soft footsteps crossing to the bell tower room. The stone angel still smiled its wreck of a smile, leaning back a little as if to rest its broken wings on the lap rug kindly left there. An hour later, Black Nightgown—the one-and-the-same old gentleman—as thoughtfully careless as before, left the heavy iron key in the West Door's lock. Outside, the great makeshift gate in the Close scraped and groaned as it was pushed shut behind the last cart and workman.

The shimmer, almost more not-there than there, rested one step down from the landing. No tea chest waited on the other side.

Later James would remember—or would think he remembered—that his heart both leaped and sank in that sliver of a second it took for his eyes to tell his mind, *No tea chest*.

It was a simple matter to sit on the stone step, to swing his legs down, to duck his head, and slip downward. Slip through. Slip away.

In the basement James edged his way through the darkness, reaching out for stair rail or wall as he went. Meeting the railing, he stepped up to feel for the light cord, found it, and pulled it. In the quick glare of light he saw everything in its place: rubbish bins, tea chests neatly stacked in the corner, and the cleaning-up rag hanging stiffly dry over the rim of the sink. That meant no clock was wrapped up in it, and so of course no clock hidden behind the boiler.

James looked in the rubbish bins. Empty, just as they had been in March.

He started up toward the door, intending to take a look into the hallway to find out whether it was day or night. There might be letters, too, to give some clue to the date. He reached out for the doorknob.

He had barely touched it when the light bulb gave a faint *pop!* and went dark.

And the doorknob turned under his fingers.

The boy who stood facing him, eyes heavy-lidded as a sleepwalker's, wore a pair of striped cotton pajamas and carried a pair of sneakers in one hand.

He stood, blinking sleepily, too startled, too baffled even to shape the question *What am I seeing?* to himself.

"It's all right." James smiled at him as he said it, and reached out his hand to catch the other's wrist as swiftly as he would to snatch a moth out of the air.

And then he was alone in the doorway.

Facing down the hallway toward the front door.

In his striped pajamas, with his sneakers in his left hand.

twenty-one

JAMES GASPED. FOR A MOMENT HE COULD NOT BREATHE, and when he could it was the shallow in-and-out of shock. He stared down at his hands, at the dangling sneakers and then at his bare feet on the cold slate tile of the hallway. At ankles that had no flea bites from the fleas in the rushes on Mrs. Matcham's floors . . .

He had thought . . . He had expected . . . When he had thought about it, he saw himself coming back like a traveler from another world in his brown jerkin and funny knee-length breeches and cloak. . . .

But this was fine. This was good. . . . This was better.

He was trembling.

He climbed the stairs slowly, his hand floating along the oak handrail in a long caress. Had he brought a key with him on those first two visits to the base-ment? He couldn't remember. It was too long ago. Too much had happened. He felt in his pajama pocket. No. But he had got back in the first two times, so he must have left the door unlocked.

On the top landing he switched off the stairwell lighting and stood for a moment looking up through the skylight at the almost-full moon. *No stars*, he thought a little sadly. The sky was too city-lit for stars. He turned the doorknob gently and eased the door open. All was quiet. He switched on the little lamp on the hall table and padded into the sitting room to pick up the clock from the middle bookshelf. He brought it out to the light.

2:27 A.M. 3 June. Tuesday.

The first night, then.

He was desperately thirsty. Going into the kitchen, he switched on the little light above the sink, took down a glass from the cupboard shelf, and filled it from the filtered-water pitcher. He drained it to the bottom, remembering the faint unpleasant smell of the diamond-cold water from the well and from the giant pitchers the water-sellers carried to fill the cisterns at the

Moults' and Blackfriars kitchen and Mrs. Matcham's.

He was home. In a world with French toast and pitchers of orange juice, and thin-crust pizza, and bread that wasn't heavy as a stone, and . . .

At his parents' bedroom door he stopped. *And his mama and dad.* James's hand reached out to the doorknob, but he drew it back. Then before the thought could shape itself again, his hand had opened the door on its own and he was standing at the foot of his parents' bed. Phil was sleeping stretched out straight on one side with his feet wound up in the sheet in the way a fork winds up spaghetti. Reenie was sprawled half on her face with one knee drawn up and her arms flung wide. They slept.

"I love you," James said aloud. Quite loud.

Reenie's left arm gave a weak flap like a half-dead fish. "Uhv yuh doo, unny," she mumbled into her pillow.

His bed was uncomfortable. Unnervingly jigglish. Too soft. He began to cry silently, tears of relief and regret sliding down his nose and cheek and into his pillow until exhaustion and the end of three weeks' terror and delight freed him, and dropped him in at the deep end of sleep.

twenty-two

"SIR? YOUR BREAKFAST, SIR."

James stirred awake to the smell of bacon and scrambled eggs and opened his eyes to see his father standing over him with an old-fashioned wicker breakfast-in-bed tray.

"Wha' time is it?" James peered at his watch. Nine o'clock!

"Mom left for the rehearsal hall half an hour ago," Phil said. "I was going to roll you out of bed when her taxi came, but she said to let you enjoy your jet lag."

James sat up and stretched his arms up over his head. "I don't think I have any. Um-m. Just Time lag."

"Same thing." His father raised the tray. "Do you want your bacon and eggs and toast here or in the kitchen? I thought we might do some sightseeing to celebrate your first day in London. If we do, the sooner out the door the better. Which'll it be? Here or there?"

"There," James said hastily. If he meant to avoid going through the past three weeks—or however much it added up to—all over again, the sooner he started changing things the better. He swung his legs out of bed and followed his father.

"There's a lot of London I've always been too busy to see myself," Phil said as he put the plate and a glass of orange juice in front of James at the breakfast table. "I thought we could take a ride on one of the open-top tour buses, then start off at Madame Tussaud's Wax Museum." He handed James a knife and fork and napkin.

"I dunno," James said quickly. "I was thinking about the Museum of London. And this afternoon there's something I'd like to look for, for Granddad." He would, he'd decided, buy the kit version of the little Zulu holding a shield and a rifle and would paint it himself. Maybe get the book on the Battle of Isandlwana in the Zulu War in South Africa, too.

His dad looked faintly puzzled. "Did I tell you

about the Museum of London? I forgot. Sure. We can do that. I had it in mind we might go there last, though, after you had some idea about where things are in the city."

"But maybe it will make things more interesting if I know something before I see it all," James answered.

"Makes sense," Phil said. He wandered over to the coffeepot on the kitchen island and poured himself a second cup. "Dennis Cross, an old friend of your mom's and mine, teaches music theory at the Guildhall School in the Barbican. If he's around maybe he can have lunch with us afterward at the Waterside Café. . . ."

James finished his second piece of toast. He guessed from his father's preoccupied look that he was trying to work out whether this meant he needed to rethink more than his first day's plans. He generally composed the expeditions on his days-out-as-father as seriously as if they were movements in a concerto: *allegro moderato, adagio, presto.* Moderately quick, slow, quick . . .

James's eyes flew open as the thought made a leap.

Maybe that was why his dad, the Mad Organizer, loved jazz. It let him fly. It set him free, because jazz could improvise from any melody, leap into the air from anywhere.

That's why he loves Mama. She lets him fly. . . .

Startled by this peculiar thought, James hastily took his plate and glass and cutlery to the dishwasher and closed it up again.

"I'll go get dressed," he said, but he had a frog in his throat and the words came out a little gargled.

"Fine," his dad replied vaguely.

Odd. James tried while he was brushing his teeth to remember what the weather had been like that first full day in London—and could not. Afterward a look out the window told him it was sunny, but not bright, so he put on a pair of jeans instead of shorts, and a new T-shirt that read **GO HERMIONE!** His mama or one of his grandmothers must have bought it for a joke and probably made bets that he would never wear it, but he thought it was funny. The lightweight clothes felt strange, though. He found himself wishing again that he could have come back in his other clothes, even if they were the crimson livery and not the suit he thought of as his . . . just to keep them hidden somewhere.

Nothing left. Not even the flea bites . . .

James went suddenly cold. *But then how could there be?*

There couldn't. Not if he really stayed away from the basement and steered clear of the Millennium Bridge. If he would not—did not dare—go back, then none of it was going to happen. If he was never going to fall into the river, then *already* none of it *had* happened. At all.

So why could he remember it?

He was as sure that he did remember it, and had not dreamed it all, as he was that up was up and down was down. But why could he, if it never happened? A one-time fluke? Not likely. He remembered wondering once which James would end up as the one-and-only official James, and thinking that he, this "he," had become—well, more *James* than the one who stepped onto the bridge that day. If you closed one eye and forgot about being logical, maybe that was it: of the two of him, the James who vanished was a pretty invisible James to start with. On the other hand, if now all he remembered never happened, the only other solution must be . . .

No. The only other solution was to get moving. If scientists wrote books and argued about Time and wormholes and alternate realities, James Hackaday Parrett wasn't going to figure it out while pulling up his socks. He tied the laces on his sneakers and hurried out into the hallway, where his dad waited.

"All this is new to me," Phil said, as they arrived at the upper-level entrance to the Museum. "This part used to be a big Nothing Much. I like it."

James nodded, but he was too impatient to get inside, to find some trace, some record of the London he knew, even to see what his dad was looking at.

"Hah, this part looks familiar," his dad said once they were past the new entry.

James saw that they had entered on the top level, and going to look over the nearby railing into a large central area, saw a courtyard garden and more galleries below. The displays on the upper level began with "London Before London" and prehistoric settlements and kept on going. Phil had seen most of it before, but stopped to peer at this and that and read the explanations, so James soon left him behind. He was slowed down only by the models of a busy riverfront dock scene and one of buildings in Roman London that his granddad would have loved. He hurried past the Roman living room and kitchen, through the Middle Ages, and into Tudor London. There he walked back and forth in a daze from one glass case to another. He saw pewter spoons like the ones he ate with. A pottery beaker for ale. A goblet exactly like Mr. Moult's. A little leather-covered glass inkwell that might have been his own. It hurt to look at them. *Four hundred years . . .*

He liked the models, though a couple were so old and grimy that he thought they needed new ones. Another old one, of the City from the river, looked wrong. The river-edge wall was missing in one stretch, and Blackfriars wasn't there. It did show the square-towered St. Paul's he knew, but with an unfamiliar spire, but afterward he saw a painting dated 1630 that showed it without the spire, exactly as he'd seen it— except that the painter had a little goofily scrunched both it and the city up a bit to fit it all in.

But . . .

He found his answer in a darkened little mini-theatre where a recorded voice read an eyewitness account while lighting effects and a model of the city showed how in 1666 a fire in a bakery became a firestorm that burned for five days. Few died, but four-fifths of the city was destroyed. *Eighty-nine churches.* Though the rebuilding began at once, many Londoners spent the winter camped in fields outside the walls.

1666. Boys he had known would have been old men. . . .

James pushed aside the dark curtain and fled the tiny theatre. He felt sick. His London had been swept away. Everyone he knew there was dead. Had been for hundreds of years. Even if he was tempted to risk going back again, now he never could. How could you bear to talk with, sing with, touch people you knew were dead? *Would be* dead. If he had stayed, he would be dead now, too.

He found his father still in Roman London, hands clasped behind his back, peering at an oil lamp shaped like a foot. "Dad? Can we go?"

Straightening, Phil gave him a sharp look. "Yes, sure."

He led the way quickly through the maze of displays and out to the museum café, where he bought a mug of tea for each of them and a packet of chocolate-filled wafers for James. They sat and drank in silence.

"Feeling better?" Phil asked when their cups were empty.

"Yes, thanks."

"Do you want to go back in?"

"No." James shook his head. "Some other time, maybe."

They took the walkway high above the street level. At first all Phil could do was marvel at how much the view of the City had changed since the last time he had come that way, and that more new tall buildings out of science-fiction fantasy were still going up. But then he stopped to lean on the railing on the other side of the walkway and look at James.

"What was it, Jimmy?" he said gently. "What upset you?"

James hesitated. "All those things. People holding them. Using them. Eating. Singing. Telling jokes. You can almost hear them. And they're all dead. All of them."

Phil took a while to answer. "You're right. It's sad. Sometimes tremendously sad. But you're feeling that because for that moment you've known they really *were alive*. Like you. Not just dusty names or statistics in a history book . . . James? What is it?"

James was staring back and forth from the green lawn and gardens stretched out below them between the buildings to the metal plaque fastened to the railing where they stood.

"The City Wall," he croaked. "It's still there! And over where the cars are parked? The diagram here says 'Monkwell Square'!"

And the high City Wall *was* there, in ruins, but still itself. Almost directly below was the high shell of one of the towers spaced out along it, and according to the diagram two others still stood, out of sight beyond the trees and shrubs.

"Right." Phil was a little startled. He could understand a bit of excitement, even awe, over a wall with parts almost two thousand years old, but—a parking area named Monkwell Square?

Farther on along the "highwalk," past shops and around a corner, they came into the giant Barbican complex with its thousands of flats, theatre, concert hall, restaurants, galleries, library, and schools. There, above eye level at the corner of a row of front doors to flats, was a sign like a street sign: THE POSTERN. James stopped dead in the middle of the walkway.

"What is it, James? You look like you've seen another ghost."

"You could say so," James said shakily, but then he took a deep breath and gave his father an unexpected smile. "Look, can you tell me where the restaurant is so I can meet you there? I want to go back and look at the Wall."

"Come, I'll show you."

The walkway, open on one side, continued along

one block of flats, then through another, and ended where it met a wider walkway. Phil kept right on to the low parapet ahead and pointed out to James the Guildhall School at ground level several storeys below. It stood directly beyond a long, broad pool, with gardens to the right. Massive blocks of flats rose all around.

"See the tables on the terrace over to the left? They belong to the Waterside Café. To get there you cross that bridge—" He pointed. "Then turn left down the ramp. You take the ramps all the way down to ground level, go through the doors, and left into the café. Twenty minutes? Say half an hour."

James went no farther than the corner on the walkway that bore the sign THE POSTERN.

The brief flash of a scene that he thought he had seen there had not been an illusion. From a narrow stretch of parapet between the corner of the building and an open stairwell leading down to the levels below, he had a clear view of a long, narrow lawn and garden at the rear of the long, outermost block of flats. At the lawn's far end stood the shell of the corner

276

tower of the old City Wall. From it, the wall itself marched along toward him to vanish from sight behind the building his shoulder leaned against. Below on the near side ran green lawn; on the far side was the old City ditch—and beyond it the church of St. Giles Cripplegate! *Still.*

It was all there . . . and not there. The stretch of City ditch so lovingly preserved now held clean water, and only parts of St. Giles's looked really old. But they were still *there.* He could almost see the ghosts of the vanished houses. A part of the green grass lawn and the adjoining halves of the middle flats of the block were Mr. Speght's school; the left-hand halves of those flats were the alley and Mr. Moult's house. The lost houses at the far end had belonged to a Mr. Beastney. Mr. Beastney, according to Mr. Moult, had built his study and bedroom inside the tower in the wall, which the boys—or at least James—had thought was cool. James's heart thumped. He could feel them all, alive still, ghosts or no. The City had burned to ashes and grown again, but it had not erased its old streets, or straightened them. They were the map of its past. Wheels still ran and feet still hurried in their ancient paths.

He stood for a long while, watching a small girl play with a black-and-white spaniel on green grass below that had been the fenced-in space where Mr. Speght's pupils played their games, and then he turned and crossed back through the postern and over the City ditch to meet his father.

That evening, on the way back to the flat from dinner at Smith's in Smithfield, the Parretts turned up St. John's Street—the shortest way to Clerkenwell Road—and James had his next-to-last surprise of the day. There, in the middle of the way, sat St. John's Gate. The real thing. A car driving through its broad arch. The window of the great chamber over the arch glowing golden with lamplight in the late summer dusk. The same great chamber where the Children had played out their play for Sir Edmund Tilney, the Master of the Queen's Revels . . .

After that, it was no surprise to see the handsome sign beside the shabby door on Clerkenwell Road:

Euan & Gillian January, Lutemakers, Second Floor.

"Lutemakers?" Phil stopped and turned back. The windows above were dark.

James could not resist. "You can come over tomor—tomorrow morning." He cleared his throat. "I bet they're nice. Tell them you're going to make me a lute."

Phil's amazed *"What?"* was lost in Reenie's crow of laughter.

"James, honey, didn't you just hear yourself? Your *voice* is cracking!"

James looked at her in disbelief and when she nodded, eyes laughing, he astonished them both by taking a running hop ahead and turning a cartwheel on the pavement.

About time!

Author's Note

Almost everyone but the Parretts, the Garlands, and Mrs. Matcham in *The Black Canary* is a real person—Master Giles, Mr. Robinson, Mr. Evans, Ben Jonson, Dr. Bull, Mr. Browne, the boys (including Jack Frost), the Duke of Essex. Mr. Moult and his house are—were—real, but I do not know what he did for a living. He *might* have been a teacher. Young Thomas Clifton truly was kidnapped at the Master's order and rescued by his determined father just as in the story. The Well I describe, the streets, the gates of the City of London, the houses, the Blackfriars theatre, Essex House, and the queen's Banqueting House, are all as they were.

And sadly, the proud, foolish Duke of Essex was executed for treason only weeks later, in February of 1601.